"You don... I'm Troy Cramer."

Sadie's mouth fell open.

"Kind of an amazing transformation, isn't it?"

You can say that again, Sadie thought. He was tall. He was muscular. And there wasn't a pocket protector in sight. A tingle began to tiptoe through her and Sadie almost gasped. She was attracted to Troy Cramer! The computer nerd! The kid most likely to be a millionaire before his twenty-fifth birthday.

Come to think of it, he had met his goal and surpassed it. She cleared her throat, not wanting to be impolite, but also not eager to stand around and drool over the most eligible bachelor in town. Because that was something the old Sadie would have done. The new Sadie didn't base her self-worth on her looks and dating the most eligible guy in town. The new Sadie wanted to be respected for her brains and abilities. The new Sadie began to walk away....

Daycare
DADS

Baby on Board (SR #1639)
The Tycoon's Double Trouble (SR #1650)
The Nanny Solution (SR #1662)

Dear Reader,

Spend your rainy March days with us! Put on a pot of tea (or some iced tea if you're in that mood), grab a snuggly blanket and settle in for a day of head-to-toe-warming— guaranteed by reading a Silhouette Romance novel!

Seeing double lately? This month's twin treats include *Her Secret Children* (#1648) by Judith McWilliams, in which our heroine discovers her frozen eggs have been stolen—and falls for her babies' father! Then, in Susan Meier's *The Tycoon's Double Trouble* (#1650), her second DAYCARE DADS title, widower Troy Cramer gets help raising his precocious daughters from an officer of the law—who also threatens his heart....

You might think of giving your heart a workout with some of our other Romance titles. In *Protecting the Princess* (#1649) by Patricia Forsythe, a bodyguard gets a royal makeover when he poses as the princess's fiancé. Meanwhile, the hero of Cynthia Rutledge's *Kiss Me, Kaitlyn* (#1651) undergoes a "make*under*" to conceal he's the company's wealthy boss. In Holly Jacobs's *A Day Late and a Bride Short* (#1653), a fake engagement starts feeling like the real thing. And while the marriage isn't pretend in Sue Swift's *In the Sheikh's Arms* (#1652), the hero never intended to fall in love, not when the union was for revenge!

Be sure to come back next month for more emotion-filled love stories from Silhouette Romance. I know I can't wait!

Mary-Theresa Hussey

Mary-Theresa Hussey
Senior Editor

Please address questions and book requests to:
Silhouette Reader Service
U.S.: 3010 Walden Ave., P.O. Box 1325, Buffalo, NY 14269
Canadian: P.O. Box 609, Fort Erie, Ont. L2A 5X3

The Tycoon's Double Trouble

SUSAN MEIER

Daycare
DADS

SILHOUETTE *Romance*®

Published by Silhouette Books

America's Publisher of Contemporary Romance

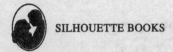

SILHOUETTE BOOKS

ISBN 0-373-19650-4

THE TYCOON'S DOUBLE TROUBLE

Books by Susan Meier

SUSAN MEIER

is one of eleven children, and though she has yet to write a book about a big family, many of her books explore the dynamics of "unusual" family situations, such as large work "families," bosses who behave like overprotective fathers, or "sister" bonds created between friends. Because she has more than twenty nieces and nephews, children also are always popping up in her stories. Many of the funny scenes in her books are based on experiences raising her own children or interacting with her nieces and nephews.

She was born and raised in western Pennsylvania and continues to live in Pennsylvania.

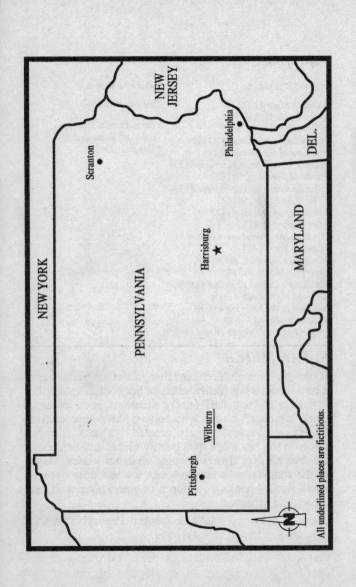

NEW YORK

NEW
JERSEY

Scranton

Philadelphia

DEL.

PENNSYLVANIA

Harrisburg

MARYLAND

Wilburn

Pittsburgh

All underlined places are fictitious.

Chapter One

Troy Cramer opened the door of his black SUV and casually stepped onto the pavement of the bank parking lot, but a flurry of movement caught his eye. Across the street, a policewoman snagged one of the local kids as he ran out the back door of Tilly's— Wilburn, Pennsylvania's answer to the 7-Eleven. Because it was clear the kid was about to be arrested, Troy waved his eight-year-old daughters to their seats, indicating they shouldn't get out of the vehicle yet. Then he caught the gaze of his daughters' bodyguard, Bruce Oliver, and made a motion with his eyes for him to take note of the scene, before he returned his attention to the policewoman and stared in awe, equal parts stunned and enthralled. Not because of the arrest, but because of the arresting officer.

Sadie Evans, the prettiest girl in Troy's high school class, still had her trademark black hair, sexy green eyes and perfect figure. But it appeared that rather than choose a career that took advantage of her good looks, as everyone expected, she was a policewoman!

Troy watched dumbstruck as the kid cursed loudly, shrugged off Sadie's grip and ran across the street toward the bank parking lot. But Sadie was every bit as fast as the boy, and she caught him about twenty feet away from Troy.

"Come on, Mark," Sadie said to the teenager. Her chin-length hair swayed as she twisted his arm behind his back and brought him to a grinding halt. "This can go easy or this can go hard. Let's do it the easy way."

"No way! I'm not going to jail!"

"Who says you're going to jail?"

Mark stopped wrestling and peered at Sadie. "I'm not going to jail?"

"No. Technically, it's only your first offense so you won't go to jail. But you are going to be punished. Lacy Vickroy says you're shoplifting every day now. You know she just bought Tilly's from the Brennans and she can't afford your stealing. She said she's talked to you, but you don't pay any attention, and she had to stop you somehow. This is it."

"Great." The teenager huffed.

"I'm going to have the police chief take you to the borough building so Lacy can file the official complaint. Since this is your first arrest, you'll get a fine, but no jail time. But your parents will be notified and I expect this to be the end of your shoplifting."

Blatantly eavesdropping, Troy stared in awe. Watching Sadie Evans arrest someone was like seeing a Barbie doll come to life and do the job she was dressed for.

"So what do you say, Mark? You're only getting a

slap on the wrist this time. But you've got to promise to stop this.''

Mark drew a long breath. Troy held his. Mark was bigger and stronger than Sadie, and if he chose to fight for real, things could get ugly. Troy almost stepped forward to help her, but Mark said, "All right.''

As Sadie led the docile boy away, Troy continued to gape in amazement, not caring that his mouth probably hung open. Sadie had been the queen of study hall. The pretty, pampered head cheerleader never studied much, but she wasn't dumb, either. She once argued the difference between peach and coral with the art teacher by showing him two lipsticks. And her fashion shows earned enough money for the cheerleaders to get new uniforms every year. But instead of becoming a model or owning a cosmetics company, she was a police officer. Troy would be damned if he ever thought he would see this day or even one close to it.

"Dad!''

Bumped out of his thoughts by his eight-year-old daughter Ginger as she whined and tugged on his hand, Troy glanced into the SUV. His little girl stared at him with crystal-clear blue eyes just like her mother's and, as always, his heart melted. "Sorry, Ginger.''

"You said we were going to pick up Grandma and go to the mall.''

"And we will, Rosemary," Troy said, his gaze sliding to his second daughter, who was identical to her twin sister. Ginger and Rosemary. Named after spices because his wife, Angelina, had thought children were the spice of life, and after thirty hours of labor, Troy hadn't argued. Then, after two weeks of being a dad, he had understood what Angelina had meant. The girls changed their lives. They made days more interesting, and certainly more challenging, but they also made every moment more special. They added meaning and purpose Troy didn't know life could have.

From that moment on, Troy had known Angelina had had an innate, uncompromising sense of what was important, and he'd never again argued when she got a certain passionate look on her face. Eighteen months past her death, he still missed that look. Still missed her.

"But first we have to get money from the bank."

"Why didn't we just use the drive-thru?" Ginger asked with a very adult sigh.

Troy grimaced. "Because I wanted to take two minutes to talk with Mr. Johnson."

"Ah, Dad!"

"Honey, I have to do this. I have to shift some of my business accounts to the bank because I'm going to need lots of money to move my company here and I'm the only one from Sunbright in Wilburn," he said, referring to his software company, Sunbright Software Solutions. "Everybody else is still in California."

"Daaaadd!"

This time both girls whined. In stereo. Troy glanced at Bruce who was sitting behind the steering wheel of the SUV. Tall and muscular, dressed in jeans and a T-shirt, Bruce looked like a normal twenty-five-year-old who probably should have reacted to the disagreement around him. But he didn't say a word. He didn't even roll his eyes or purse his lips.

Troy knew why. In the months since the death of the girls' mother, Troy had pampered his twins. No. He had spoiled them. Undoubtedly, Bruce had grown

accustomed to it. But though Bruce was too polite to
say it, or even acknowledge it, Troy had long ago
begun noticing he was creating little monsters out of
his daughters.

In fact, that was why he had moved them to his
hometown of Wilburn, Pennsylvania, population
4,500. First, it was safer, quieter, calmer than L.A. any
day of the week. Second, he was hoping that if his
twins saw the way normal people behaved, eventually
they would take the hint and change.

Even after six months, no such luck.

"Okay, let's compromise. I won't open the accounts
right now. I'll just tell Mr. Johnson to expect me in
about two hours. But that means we cut your mall trip
short."

Ginger sighed with disgust. Rosemary crossed her
arms on her chest and looked away. Troy prayed for
strength. But he suddenly got a flash of memory of
Sadie Evans as a teenager crossing her arms on her
chest exactly the same way and pouting prettily, and
he burst out laughing. The truth was he was raising
two little Sadies. Which was funny until he guessed
that he was probably in for at least ten more years of
this kind of behavior. No, he *knew* he had ten more
years of this kind of behavior, because when he left
town right after high school graduation, Sadie hadn't
changed a bit. Somewhere between age eighteen and
twenty-eight she had performed a miracle, but she
hadn't done it before eighteen, which meant Troy
could be in for a long, difficult decade.

"Come on," he said, motioning the girls out of the
SUV. "The sooner we get done in the bank, the sooner
we get to the mall."

"Whatever," Ginger grumbled, and Troy bit back

a sigh, catching Bruce's gaze. Again, Bruce didn't react. Not because he didn't understand what was going
on, but because it wasn't his job to interfere. But Troy
knew somebody had to interfere. He couldn't take ten
more years of this. Worse, he knew that if he didn't
soon think of a way to reach his daughters, they would
spend their next year at Briarhills School for Young
Ladies in detention.

As the girls piled out of the SUV, Bruce also
stepped out. But he didn't accompany the Cramer family into the bank. Instead, he sat on the park bench on
the sidewalk out front, quietly monitoring the scene
on Main Street. With his nondescript haircut and low-
key demeanor, Bruce looked like any other guy taking
a break on the sunny August afternoon. Just the way
Troy wanted it. Though his normal life disappeared
with his wife's death, Troy kept his protection efforts
low-key. His chief of security blended in as much as
possible, acting as the cook when they were at the
mansion, the driver when they were in the car and a
family friend when the girls walked around the mall.

Troy led his daughters through the glass door and
immediately strode to the receptionist's desk. He
handed Amelia Wirfel his check to be cashed and
asked to see Mr. Johnson. He didn't waste his time
with automatic teller machines. He had more money
in this bank than all the other residents of the town
combined. He was also moving his software business
to Wilburn, which eventually meant moving a good
deal of his company's money to the bank, too. So he
didn't think anyone expected him to stand in line. In
fact, he would bet it surprised most people to see he
did his own banking. But until he moved his staff to
Wilburn, he was alone—except for Jake Malloy, a

friend from high school who had become his private investing partner.

"Troy!" Ray Johnson said, his voice booming through the hollow first floor of the brick lobby. The barrel-chested bank manager barely concealed his eagerness as he bounded across the ceramic floor to intercept Troy. "How are you, son?"

"I'm fine, Mr. Johnson. You remember my daughters?"

"Of course, I do," Ray said, bending to pat Ginger's cheek. Troy prayed she wouldn't turn her head and bite him. When Ray pulled his hand back and had all five fingers, Troy smiled with relief.

"How are you, girls?"

"Fine, Mr. Johnson," they said in unison, sounding like stereo again, but at least not sounding like bored little divas.

"I'm waiting for Amelia to get me some cash," Troy said to Ray. "But I also wanted to see if you were free this afternoon to help me create the accounts I'm going to need to facilitate the transfer of my company to Wilburn."

"Of course! Of course!" Ray boomed, gesturing broadly toward his office. "We'll open an account and make arrangements for the wire transfer right now."

Rosemary shot Troy a warning look, and Troy felt his pulse rate pick up. This was getting ridiculous. He could understand the pouting and even the whining, but expressions of reprimand and warning were new. And a sign that unless he did something, things would get worse before they got better.

Still, this wasn't the time or the place to address it. "Actually, I'm busy for the next two hours, but I'll be back."

"I can accommodate you now," Ray assured Troy.

Troy shook his head. "No. That's okay. Two hours from now is fine."

"Very good," Ray said, just as Amelia returned with Troy's cash.

Troy smiled at Amelia. "Thanks."

"You're welcome," she said, bestowing upon Troy a beautiful smile that Troy hardly noticed. Well, he noticed but he didn't *notice*. Not the way he soaked in every detail about Sadie. But Sadie was different. Troy had had a crush on her in high school, but every guy did. Reacting to her smile, her hair or her sexy green eyes was second nature.

The minute they stepped out of the bank, Bruce rose from the bench and became part of the group walking up the sidewalk to the rear parking lot.

Troy turned to Rosemary. "Exactly what was that look about?"

She blinked at him. "What?"

"Don't give me 'what.' You looked at me funny in there. You reprimanded me."

"We're just tired of waiting, Dad," Ginger said, explaining, Troy knew, to save her sister. It was always like this with them. There were two of them and one of him. And most of the time one of them played arbiter. Which meant most of the time they won the arguments.

Of course, it didn't help that Troy was a softie with them because they looked like his late wife and they were growing up without their wonderful mother. Troy missed Angelina with the misery and sadness of a man who knew he would probably spend the rest of his life alone. But the girls were missing a mother. A female influence. Somebody to watch and emulate.

They turned the corner toward the bank parking lot, and Troy saw Chief Tom Marshall guiding Mark toward the borough building, which housed offices for the police, the water authority, the mayor and the town council. Sadie stayed behind, standing in front of Tilly's, talking with two wide-eyed teenage girls. He couldn't hear what anybody was saying, but he could see that the kids were confiding in her, trusting her. About what, Troy didn't have a clue, but when she put her hand on the shoulder of the first girl, Troy knew his instinct was correct. She had a rapport with them. When the girl stepped forward and hugged Sadie in response, Troy knew his second instinct was correct. They trusted her.

"Daaaad!"

"Sorry," he said, realizing he was watching Sadie again. He couldn't help but remember that years ago Sadie had been exactly like his twins, yet here she stood, a mature, trusted adult. As that thought blossomed in his brain, he had another thought, more like a flash of brilliance. It was so powerful that he stopped dead in his tracks.

She was a trusted adult. With the exception of her looks, everything about her was the opposite of high school. Which meant the very last thing she wanted was to marry a rich man—since she had listed that as her life goal in her yearbook quote. So she could not only be the mature adult for his daughters to emulate, but also he could approach her for help without worry of her motives.

It was perfect!

"Daaaad!"

This time Troy didn't answer his daughters. He reached into his pocket for his cell phone and began dialing. "Mom?" he said when his mother answered her phone. "I'm at the bank and something's come up. Could you take the girls to the mall without me? Great. We'll be waiting for you in the parking lot. See you in five minutes."

Before Troy could return to the SUV, Bruce walked up beside him and quietly said, "What's this?"

"I have something I need to do. You're going to have to cover for me at the mall."

Bruce planted his tongue in his cheek and said, "It'll be the thrill of my week."

"I'm sure," Troy began, but Ginger gaped at him. "You're not coming?"

"Don't worry. I'll give Grandma the cash and two of my credit cards. But no snakeskin, no boas and no makeup."

"Daaaaad!"

This time Troy issued the warning look. "Don't push me."

When the handsome man fell in step beside Sadie Evans as she approached the borough building, she hardly paid any attention—except to observe that he was incredibly good-looking. Sandy brown hair fell boyishly to his forehead. Dark blue eyes accented his angular face. His body shape was somewhere between thin and muscular. He had the type of physique most women considered absolutely perfect. She would have to be blind not to notice him, even though she was sure it was a coincidence they were in step.

But when he said, "So, what happened with Mark?" Sadie knew it wasn't an accident they were going in the same direction. "Mark?"

"The kid I saw you arrest for shoplifting."

"I'm really not at liberty to talk about that."

"I don't want to know about the crime. I want to know about how you did what you did. How you learned to talk to teenagers so well. I saw Mark try to get away. I heard you talk him out of it. And I'm interested to hear about how you do it."

She peered at him but didn't stop walking. "What are you? Some kind of police junkie?"

"No, I'm just curious." He paused, gave her a funny look, then smiled broadly. "You don't remember me, do you?"

Sadie studied the absolutely gorgeous man walking beside her and had to admit that he was right. She didn't remember him, but that made her think she didn't know him at all. There was no way she would forget the thick lashes surrounding his very blue eyes, his nearly perfect face and his very trim, very toned, very sexy body. If she had met him, she was sure she should have remembered him. Which meant he was lying, trying to get her to believe she knew him so she would talk to him.

Still, rather than create a scene, she shrugged and said, "Sorry. Don't remember you."

"You don't remember how you held court in sixth-period study hall?"

She stopped walking and peered at him again. Only someone who had been in high school with her would know about her legendary study halls.

"Let me put you out of your misery," he said, then he laughed and extended his hand. "I'm Troy Cramer."

Her mouth fell open. It fell so fast and so hard, she felt it bounce. *This* was Troy Cramer.

"Kind of an amazing transformation, isn't it?"

You can say that again, Sadie thought. He was tall. He was muscular. He was gorgeous. And there wasn't a pocket protector anywhere in sight.

"They say men don't mature until they're in their twenties, and I guess I could be the poster child for that theory."

"Right," Sadie said, finally finding her voice. "I'm sorry. But you really look different."

"I'm going to take that as a compliment."

"No offense to your high school self, but you *should* take it as a compliment."

He laughed, and the sound seemed to seep into her bloodstream and resonate through her. Not only was he gorgeous, but he had a wonderful, deep voice. And beautiful eyes, she thought, unable to tear her gaze from them. They were so dark and so perfect she couldn't believe he hid them behind Coke-bottle glasses in high school. And that mouth. Full and wide. Soft and pliant-looking…

A tingle began to tiptoe through her, and Sadie almost gasped. She was attracted to Troy Cramer! The computer nerd! The kid voted most likely to be a millionaire before his twenty-fifth birthday.

Come to think of it, he had met that goal and surpassed it. She recalled her mother saying at dinner the other day that Troy Cramer's software company had made him a billionaire, but when his wife died, he had left L.A. to raise his daughters in a quieter environment. Her mother also said how the people of the town rarely saw him because he ran his California-based company from his home and that he worked twelve to sixteen hours a day. Which made Troy Cramer rich, good-looking, available and probably very lonely.

She cleared her throat, not wanting to be impolite

but also not eager to stand around and drool over the most eligible bachelor in town. That was something the old Sadie would have done. The new Sadie did not base her self-worth on her looks and dating the most eligible guy in town. The new Sadie wanted to be respected for her brains and abilities. The new Sadie began to walk away from him.

"I really have to be going, but it was nice to see you. Maybe on my next trip home, we'll run into each other again."

She didn't plan to run into him, see him or even talk to him again if she could help it, but there was no reason to be rude.

"You don't live in Wilburn?"

Sadie stopped. "Actually, I do live in Wilburn." She smiled sheepishly. "I keep forgetting that because I just moved home from Pittsburgh last week."

"Oh."

His tone clearly told her he was happy about that. He smiled at her, and little pinpoints of awareness spiked all over her body. But she ignored them because it was foolish to be attracted to him. If she got involved with Troy Cramer, it would be like high school all over again, and she'd be the talk of the town. Then, instead of gaining the respect she hoped to gain by doing a great job as a member of the town's police force, she would be back to being pretty, pampered Sadie, the idiotic high school senior who announced in the class yearbook that she intended to marry someone with more money and smaller ears than Prince Charles.

Oh, no. She wasn't going back to that!

"I just liked the way you handled arresting Mark. Made me feel all safe inside."

Sadie laughed. "Funny. Very, very funny."

"That was *my* high school trademark."

"I remember," she said as unexpected memories of him as a sweet, considerate and extremely funny teenager flooded her thoughts. They hadn't been in each other's social circle, but they had been biology lab partners sophomore year.

"And yours was being pretty."

"Right." Normally that comment would make her bristle, but she gave Troy the benefit of the doubt since he hadn't seen her in over ten years and wouldn't realize comments like that drove her nuts. "Like you said, we all grow up sometime."

"But you grew up *really well.*"

Knowing she had to go before he unintentionally made her mad, Sadie said, "Thanks. But since you grew up *really well,* too, that only means we're even."

With that Sadie pivoted and tried again to walk away, but he said, "No, we're not. My transformation was physical. I still went and did what everyone expected of me, but you've really changed the direction of your life. Your transformation was personal. Emotional. And I'll bet you've worked very hard at it."

Sadie stopped, compelled to face him again. It shocked her that he recognized something her family hadn't seen, but she knew better than to turn it into a big deal. "I made a few good life choices, Troy. No need to call the Pope for a canonization."

"I wasn't thinking about calling the Pope. I wasn't even going to alert a bishop. But I might have a business proposition for you."

She laughed. "You have a business proposition for me because I grew up?" she asked skeptically.

"Exactly. You see, I have eight-year-old twin

daughters. They were devastated when their mother died.'' He paused for a second, and from the expression that quickly passed over his face, Sadie could tell he worked to hold his own reaction to that in check. ''It took me over a year to realize I needed a different kind of environment to raise them in. Once I did, we moved home.''

''That's good.'' Sadie politely nodded her understanding of at least that point, though she didn't have a clue where this discussion was going or what he wanted from her. And she was unable to think of a courteous way to walk away from a man who had just mentioned his late wife.

''But moving home really didn't help.'' He paused again, then glanced around. ''Is there somewhere more private we could talk?''

''No,'' Sadie said, recognizing her opening to leave and grabbing it. ''Because, really, Troy, I have to get going. I don't know what kind of business proposition you have for me but I can save you some trouble. I'm new in this job, and it's going to keep me very busy. I won't have time for anything else.''

''Not even if I paid you a hundred thousand dollars?''

Rich. Good-looking. Certifiable. ''What in the devil would you possibly be willing to pay me a hundred thousand dollars to do?''

''To teach my girls about being a woman.''

Though he said the statement perfectly calmly and with no undertones of anything even remotely rude, all of Sadie's defenses sprang to life. Still, because he hadn't come right out and said he wanted her to teach his daughters to be pretty and popular, and because he genuinely seemed to understand that her transformation had been an important one, she didn't let herself explode with frustration.

Instead, she took a quick breath to calm herself and asked, "What *exactly* are you talking about?"

"My girls need a woman to teach them the finer points of being feminine, things I can't teach them. But I want to make sure they're taught in the right way. I don't want them growing up thinking they can run around in feather boas and snakeskin hip huggers just because the girls in videos do. I don't want them thinking see-through blouses are acceptable. Somebody has to teach them how to dress, show them what's feminine and what's trash. I don't know how. But I do have money. So, I would be willing to pay you a hundred thousand dollars to do the job."

Finally understanding his request, Sadie sighed with relief. "Troy, you are in luck."

His lips curved upward in an alluring smile, and again Sadie felt the pull of attraction, but she expertly squelched it. She wanted to be a respected police officer. She did not want to be a billionaire's kept woman. If he didn't have all that money, she would be flirting with him to high heaven. But he did have all that money. Probably more money than she could fathom. That meant she had to stay away from him.

"You'll take the job?"

"No, but my sister Hannah will. She's an elementary-school teacher, but she also works at my aunt Sadie's day care as a single-dad instructor." She shrugged. "Your case would require tutoring a little different from her usual course material, but I can't see why Hannah couldn't adjust enough that she would be able to help you for a few weeks with your daughters."

"Your sister is a teacher?"

Sadie nodded.

He shook his head. "Not good. Not good at all. A teacher is too normal, too obvious. My girls would catch on to that too quickly. They need somebody special."

"Look, Troy, it's admirable that you want the best for your girls. But wanting the best for your daughters actually means you don't want me."

"I don't think so. You see, my wanting you to teach them has nothing to do with me wanting the best for them and everything to do with your being special. Sadie, don't you know how fabulous you are? What a role model you are? The people of the town might not see how much you've changed or might not recognize what all that changing meant, what it cost you, how much discipline you must have had…" He looked at her. Really looked at her. "But I do."

And he almost had her. Appreciation spiraled through her and nearly overruled common sense, because nobody, not one person, understood how hard she had worked to make the transition from nail-painting, hair-fluffing, only-interested-in-how-she-looked Sadie to mature Sadie. Most people didn't think it would last. Most people seemed to be waiting for her to sit on a table in the diner and hold court as she had in study hall. And the one person who seemed to understand that she had changed was the one person who was strictly off-limits.

She sighed. "Thank you. And believe me, I appreciate that you noticed how hard my transition was, but I still have to pass." She dug in her trouser pocket and pulled out a business card for the day care—one of seven her father insisted his children carry for situations just like this one.

"My aunt Sadie is sick," she said, handing Troy the card. "My sister Caro is actually running the day care, but my parents are doing the initial interviews with the applicants. If Hannah can't help you, they'll direct your case to Caro. Either Hannah or Caro would be an excellent helper for your daughters."

With that she turned away and jogged into the borough building before Troy had a chance to stop her.

Troy tapped the card against his palm, knowing that he would indeed pay a visit to the senior Evans to see about hiring someone to help him with his daughters. But it wasn't going to be Hannah. And it wasn't going to be Caro.

He wanted Sadie. He would get Sadie.

Chapter Two

"Very funny!" Furious with Troy Cramer, Sadie burst into his mansion the next morning when he answered the door. The elegant marble floors and crystal chandelier of the foyer made her feel she was walking into a museum rather than a house, but she was so angry with him even his palatial home couldn't intimidate her. "I don't know if I should sock you for being arrogant or arrest you for bribing my dad!"

"You can't arrest me. I didn't do anything illegal."

He crossed his arms on his chest. Sadie was glad she was consumed with fury because he looked gorgeous in tennis whites—tan, supple-muscled and sexy. From the appearance of his windblown hair, he had just finished his morning exercise and was probably on his way to change clothes for work. It was hard to believe someone so cute and so smart could be so thickheaded.

"I simply made a deal. The transaction wasn't even slightly shady."

"You offered a man with an ailing sister a hundred thousand dollars to get the services of his daughter. You don't call that shady?" She gaped at him as if he were crazy. "It's almost obscene!"

"Your dad said your aunt Sadie needs the money to remodel her day-care building. I need help with my twins. Where I come from this is nothing but business."

"You come from right here, Troy!"

"Yeah, well, L.A. feels more like home to me now, and in L.A. we call it business. You have what I need. I'm willing to pay for it."

"Okay," Sadie said, suddenly understanding many things simultaneously. First, his house looked like an L.A. mansion, not a museum. Second, he was very much at home in the grand house because he considered himself more a big-city person than a small-town guy. Third, that actually worked in her favor, because his being comfortable in a house that would make most people nervous proved he wasn't the same sweet, sincere guy he used to be, and she didn't have to worry about being attracted to him. His arrogance would easily overshadow his good looks and her fond memories. There was no danger of her falling for him. Not even accidentally. Which meant her biggest concern about taking this job had just been eliminated.

"I'm going to help you, but only because Aunt Sadie needs the money. So don't think you've won. There will be ground rules."

"What kind?"

"Don't say 'what kind' like a man who thinks he's negotiating. Your haggling is done. You follow my rules or you find somebody else."

Clearly confused by her anger, he frowned at her. "You're awfully prickly in the morning."

"Yeah, well, you're obnoxious when you're throwing your money around, so we're even." She drew a quick breath. "The ground rules are simple, and I'm creating them for a good reason. I'm a police officer, Troy. I easily got a job in Pittsburgh and kept it with commendations, but I couldn't get hired in Wilburn until I assisted in the Rory Brennan investigation and proved to the chief and the town council that I was competent. I want to keep this job."

"I'm not hiring you permanently. You don't have to quit the force."

"I will if everybody loses respect for me."

"Nobody's going to lose respect for you just because you're working for me."

"Oh, really? If we go public with this deal, you don't think at least some of the townspeople will gossip that I finagled this job to be close to you so I could marry you for your money?"

Troy grimaced. "Oh, right. I forgot how news travels in this town. But I do remember the gist of your yearbook quote." He paused, obviously trying to conjure up the words in his mind. "Something about marrying someone with smaller ears and a bigger bank account than Prince Charles."

Wishing her family lived in a city where people had more to entertain them than the mistakes of their neighbors, Sadie sighed. "Thanks for the recap, but the rest of the town won't need your help remembering. My first week on the job was a misery of teasing from people I hardly know. The only reason the badgering has died down is that I haven't given anyone reason to see me as anything but a very competent police officer.''

"That makes sense.''

"Yes, it does. But it also means that if everyone is going to continue to see me as a competent police officer, we need to keep my working for you a secret.''

He shrugged carelessly. "We can do that.''

"And we can't have any contact. You stay away from me. I'll stay away from you. So that if and when the story breaks, everyone will see I was only here to do a job, not to snag a husband. You can give me instructions through one of the members of your staff.''

"Are you sure you don't want to do something more, like give each other code names or maybe communicate through encrypted e-mails?''

Sadie sighed. "I'm not trying to be difficult, but you need to understand keeping my reputation is just as important to me as getting help for your daughters is to you.''

Troy laughed. "That's okay, Sadie. I understand. I only said that because I was trying to be funny.''

"You failed.''

"I'm not always at the top of my comedic game. I'm much better with computers.'' He stuck out his hand to shake hers. "Okay, here's the new deal as I see it. You teach my girls. I won't make any passes at you, and you won't make any passes at me. I'll tell my staff to keep your working here a secret, and I'll happily, very gratefully pay your aunt's day care a hundred thousand dollars for your services.''

Sadie took the hand he had extended. The second their palms brushed, awareness shivered through her. She ignored it. She had to. If she even smiled at him in the company of another person, the story would get blown out of proportion, and that yearbook quote would pop up everywhere she went. Louis would probably print the damned thing on the diner place mats. Reverend Barnes would make her the unnamed example of his next Jezebel sermon. Merely by being at Troy's house, she risked her reputation, and she wasn't even sure she could do what he wanted.

Before she released Troy's hand and sealed the deal, she said, "You never did spell out what my services would be."

"I just want the girls to spend time with you. You know, have casual conversations that lead to you subtly pointing them in the right direction about clothes, makeup and boys. I don't want you to discipline them or lecture them. I just want you to befriend them, show them a good example."

"Okay," Sadie said, giving his hand a firm shake. "It's a deal."

"Deal."

"How long am I supposed to do this?" Sadie asked, absently wiping her hand on the thigh of her jeans trying to get rid of the tingle.

"School starts in three weeks. I don't think you'll need more than a couple of hours a day every day for the next two weeks, but we have that third week as a cushion just in case."

"Good." Sadie glanced around uneasily. Two or three weeks she could handle. "So, where are your girls?"

"Upstairs. I'll…"

She shook her head. "No. You grab your golf cart and drive yourself to another wing of the mansion or something," she said, referring to the fact his house was ridiculously enormous. "Because that's how people have no contact. They don't do things together. That's why I said we would communicate through members of your staff. Send somebody else to help me find your daughters' room."

"Okay," Troy said cautiously. "But the thing of it is, I wasn't expecting you this morning, so I haven't mentioned any of this to the girls."

"If you're nervous about your daughters meeting me, don't be. I'm not as good with kids as Hannah and Caro, but I'm not a complete novice. Every morning, your twins and I will swim together. Having something to do will loosen us up and help us get to know each other so talking will be easy."

Hesitant, but somewhat trapped because he needed her enough that he had to let her call at least some of the shots, Troy agreed. "Okay. There are swimsuits in the pool house."

She shook her head. "I don't need your suit," she said, then caught his gaze. Determination shone in her green eyes. "I brought my own."

"All right." From the expression in her eyes, Troy realized she was very serious about not being involved with him, and he was surprised at the twinge of disappointment he felt.

However, he didn't have to think too hard to figure out why. He had spent his entire high school stay nursing a crush on her, and all those feelings had returned. She was gorgeous, feisty, sexy, and if he were in the market for a relationship, she would be the first person on his list to date. But the truth was, he didn't want a relationship. Not because he didn't want a woman in his life, but because his life was odd and difficult. Bodyguards were just barely disguised as servants and lived with him and his family twenty-four hours a day, seven days a week. Angelina couldn't tolerate it. She had insisted on living as normally as possible, and it had cost her her life. He would never subject another woman to the torture of the loss of personal space and freedom. Especially not an independent woman like Sadie. The confinement would kill her. No matter how much of a crush he had on her, he wouldn't pursue her. So Sadie's suggestion that they keep their distance was for the best.

"I'll send Bruce out from the kitchen to take you to the girls."

"Good."

"Good."

He left her standing in his foyer and threaded his way through the downstairs halls and corridors to the kitchen. Sadie had caught him off guard with her unexpected early morning visit, but everything seemed to work out. Which was incredibly lucky for him, since he was more convinced than ever that he needed her. *Her.* Not her sister, not his mother, not any other woman on the face of this earth. He knew only Sadie would understand the phase his daughters were going through. The fact that she was still dodging that yearbook quote validated his theory. The girls needed to see that something they did now really could follow them into adulthood in a small town.

Troy found Bruce, outlined the situation with Sadie and told him to handle introducing her to the girls. Bruce immediately left the kitchen, and Troy headed up the back steps to take a shower. By the time he finished dressing and reached his first-floor office, Sadie and the twins were on their way to the pool.

Standing by his office window, out of range of the

camera and speaker that allowed him all-day audio and video access to his secretary in California, Troy shifted one slat of the vertical blind—just a sliver—and watched Sadie lead the girls to the swimming pool. With his twins dressed in white terry cover-ups almost identical to the one Sadie wore, and all three carrying pool toys and wearing sunglasses, they looked like a parade.

They stopped by one of the many navy blue and white flowered chaise longues that surrounded the Olympic-size pool that had just been completed. All three dumped their pool toys on the chaise. Then Sadie turned and began talking to his daughters. He could tell by the way they stared at her with rapt attention that what she was saying was important or somehow significant. All three laughed, and Sadie began removing her cover-up.

Troy's heart stopped. His daughters were about to swim with a sex goddess, and he had no idea what kind of bathing suit she had on. Stories about her swimming attire from years ago were as legendary as her study halls. True, Troy believed she had changed, but what if she hadn't? What if he had misinterpreted everything? For all he knew, she could be wearing a string bikini.

His mouth went dry, and his pulse sprang into overdrive. The dad in him froze with dread. But the male in him—the sexual part that had lusted after his high school biology lab partner—froze with anticipation, knowing he might be on the verge of seeing something spectacular.

Sadie Evans in a string bikini.

He couldn't imagine it.

He'd never dared picture it, but if his daughters

weren't the two innocents by the pool with her, he
would actually be praying for it right now.

Leaning forward, holding his breath, Troy watched
as Sadie shifted a shoulder, and one side of the terry
cloth fell to her bicep. She shifted the other shoulder,
and that section fell, too. But she stopped. With the
white garment gathered at her elbows and only half of
her naked back exposed, she listened as Ginger spoke,
gesturing wildly with her hands, as if explaining something.

Troy leaned forward again. *Come on, Ginger. Speed
it up, honey. Daddy needs to know if he should be
grabbing a blanket and running to your rescue.*

Yeah, right.

"You know, in some countries Peeping Toms are
hanged."

Troy stifled the impulse to jump two feet in the air
at the sound of Jake's voice. Instead, he turned like a
normal man with nothing to hide.

"I'm not a Peeping Tom. I hired Sadie Evans to
teach the girls a few female things. This is her first
day with them, and I want to make sure everything
goes okay."

Jake ambled into Troy's office, passing the row of
computers that lined the back wall and walking to the
chair in front of Troy's desk. A former star quarter-
back who parlayed his high school success into a college scholarship, Jake didn't wear dress pants and a
dress shirt, but a polo shirt and jeans. Tall and clas-
sically good-looking with his black hair and dark
brown eyes, Jake was one of those guys women
chased. That was part of the reason Troy liked having
him around. Troy didn't have to worry about un-
wanted female attention if Jake was in the room.

Jake fell into the chair in front of Troy's desk. "I'm sure the fact that this might be the first time either one of us sees Sadie in a swimsuit has nothing to do with your being glued to the window."

"I'm not glued to the window," Troy said as he hastily snapped off the audio-video connection to his secretary in California, not needing this conversation to ripple through her workstation and potentially into the ears of every passerby in the corporate office. "I'm a dad," he said, then subtly opened the vertical blind a fraction of an inch so he could monitor the scene outside from his desk chair. He had no intention of blatantly spying on Sadie, but he was going to see how she handled his daughters and how they handled her. "I'm concerned about the girls."

"Right. Me, too," Jake said, then he chuckled merrily and moved to the right so he could also see out the opening in the blind.

If Jake hadn't been laughing, Troy knew he would have been jealous, probably angry, and that brought him up short. He never before had a problem distancing himself from a woman. In fact, he considered himself a pro. But luckily Jake was laughing. He was laughing a lot, and usually that meant trouble.

"What are you so happy about this morning?"

Jake grinned. "I still can't believe you hired me to work for your software company."

"I'm desperate. I don't have time to coordinate this move alone, and you're available. You proved your worth in the years we've been investing together. When George Parment decided not to relocate with Sunbright, you were the logical choice to replace him."

"And I love taking your money." Apparently tired

of waiting for Sadie to remove her cover-up, or else not as interested as Troy thought, Jake sat back in his chair. "We're a match made in heaven."

"You're not taking my money. As vice president of operations, you're going to earn your keep," Troy said, his attention divided between the conversation and watching Sadie, who still clutched the terry-cloth robe to her. Clearly, his daughters had warmed up to her. They weren't starry-eyed worshipers, but Troy could see they were very happy to be in her company.

"That's actually what I came in here to talk about."

"What?" Troy asked casually, but Sadie again began sliding off her white bathing suit cover, and Troy moved slightly, turning a little more toward the window, his attention on that one small slice of white material that currently dangled around Sadie's middle.

"About the added work my new position gives me."

Let it go, Sadie. Just let it slither right down those long legs to the shiny blue and white ceramic tile.

As if hearing Troy's thoughts, Sadie released her hold on the terry-cloth robe, and it billowed to the tile. Troy leaned back in his chair, struggling to control his breathing.

Good God.

"I was busy enough researching our investments before getting the extra responsibilities of the vice presidency. Now, I'm afraid I'm not going to have enough time to do either job right."

Troy cleared his throat. "What do you think we should do?" he asked, unconsciously turning his chair completely toward the window. The black one-piece suit Sadie wore should have been conservative. It should have been sedate. It would have been sedate on any other woman, but even a dust cloth would look like spun silk against Sadie's skin, and Troy should have known better than to leave open the blind. His girls were in good hands. He knew that. He had an innate sense that he could trust Sadie. That's why he had hired her. And he had already seen confirmation that the twins liked her. It was only masochism that had him watching her, looking for trouble. And he had found it.

"I'm thinking that I should hire dancing girls for secretaries and maybe promote Bruce to CEO."

Troy barely heard what Jake said as he watched Sadie and the twins walk to the pool. Two pros, the girls didn't pause but immediately jumped in. Sadie dipped in only one toe. The muscles of her legs flexed, forming perfect calves. The muscles of Troy's stomach quivered, forming a large knot.

Luckily Jake moved, reminding Troy there was another person in the room. "Jake, you're the new vice president of operations. Make whatever changes you feel necessary."

"I'm glad you said that because I was also thinking that we should have bikini-and-beer day every Thursday, and on Friday nights we'll dress up like the cast of ER and see if any hospital will actually let us treat patients."

Sadie raised her arms and dove into the water, her body forming a perfect arc before she cut into the shimmering blue depths. Troy let out the breath he had been holding and, remembering Jake, said, "I probably should have done that years ago."

Jake burst out laughing. "Troy, you better get your eyes off Sadie Evans and get your brain in this room or you're going to miss something important."

Knowing Jake was right but not about to admit it, Troy turned from the window. "I heard everything you said."

"You just approved hiring dancing girls for secretaries, bikini-and-beer Thursdays and field trips dressed as ER doctors."

"What the hell are you talking about?"

"About the fact that you're not paying attention, and you need to. I assessed my workload now that I'm taking a job with Sunbright, and I realized I need an assistant. Not an assistant like a secretary, but another accountant. So I'm thinking we should bring somebody in as comptroller."

"Got anybody in mind?"

Jake looked him right in the eye. "Luke Evans."

Troy held back a wince. "Sadie's brother?"

"Exactly."

"Okay," Troy said, drawing out the one word as if it were two.

"And since we'll be working here from this house until we find new digs, you better figure out how to keep your eyes in your head and your tongue in your mouth every time you look at his little sister, or he's going to deck you."

"Point taken."

"Good."

"But I don't want to hire him yet."

Jake sat back in his chair. "Does that have anything to do with what I just told you?"

"Yes. Sadie's only going to be here two or three weeks. I told her it would probably take two weeks to get the girls in line, but school starts in three. If she needs that last week I want her to be able to take it."

Jake sighed with disgust. "You can control yourself for two or three weeks."

"It's not me I'm worried about." Troy nodded toward the window. "Look at her. She's perfectly normal, natural and relaxed with those girls."

"And looking sweet in that suit." Jake whistled and rose from his seat to get a closer look. "Good God."

Troy stifled the urge to sock him. "My thoughts exactly," he said, his gaze drifting to the pool area for one last longing look before he forced himself back to the point. "She's a career woman with no children, but notice how she handles kids."

"She's a natural."

"Yes. As long as she's alone, unwatched…"

Jake gave Troy a skeptical look. "Unwatched?"

"All right, alone and not knowing she's being watched. She's very, very good with kids. Yet yesterday when I saw her on the street and offered this deal to her, she told me she wasn't."

"Maybe she doesn't think she is."

"My guess is that's because she comes from a family of people who are not only gifted with kids, they work with kids both in the day-care center and as teachers. They're the experts. Because Sadie isn't trained as they are she probably feels less than competent and nervous with kids around them. So I want to keep her away from her family and her family away from her. I don't want to screw this up for any of us by bringing in someone who might make her nervous."

Jake walked back to his chair. "Your money doesn't make her nervous?"

"I think she hates my money."

"Well, there's a first."

"And not something anybody expected from Sadie. In fact, we made a few side agreements to our deal. First, I promised to keep Sadie being here a secret. That means you can't tell anybody she's working here."

Jake shrugged and nodded his agreement. "Sure."

"Second, Sadie and I agreed to stay away from each other and not have any kind of association while she's here, so people don't think she took this job to try to catch herself a husband."

"Oh, I get it," Jake said with understanding. "That's why you let yourself watch her from the window. You pretty much figure you can moon over her all you want because you know she will never make a pass at you because she's still fighting her old high school reputation." He paused, thought for a second, then said, "What was that yearbook quote?"

"Something about Prince Charles's ears."

"Yeah," Jake said, obviously remembering. "Sadie said she was going marry a Prince Charles but with smaller ears and a bigger bank account."

"What did you people do? Memorize that?"

"Didn't have to. The part about the ears sort of makes it stick in a brain." He peered at Troy. "And your ears are definitely smaller than Prince Charles's. Plus, if the rumors about the royal family are true, you've also got more money. You are in big trouble."

"Not if she's changed."

Jake crossed his arms on his chest and sat back in his chair. "You're counting on that."

Hearing Jake's serious tone, Troy realized they had gone from teasing into a real conversation, and he held Jake's gaze. "Shouldn't I?"

"She's changed. Completely."

"But…"

"But…" Jake winced. "Troy, I'm not exactly known for my diplomacy or people skills."

"Then just spit it out."

"Okay. Here goes. I know you don't want another woman in your life. I think you blame your lifestyle for your wife's death. And it all makes perfect sense to me. But if you're looking to protect yourself from a relationship by hiring somebody who can't get involved with you for her own reasons, it isn't going to work. The guarantee you're looking for doesn't have anything to do with Sadie. She is so determined to prove to the town she's changed that you could dance naked in front of the pool, and she wouldn't notice."

"Then everything should be fine."

Jake shook his head. "Everything won't be fine, because *you're* the variable. If you really don't want to get involved with a woman, whatever your reason, you shouldn't have Sadie here. You like her too much and you're a little too attracted to her."

Troy waved his hand in dismissal. "That's ridiculous. In all the time you've known me have you ever seen me lose control around a woman?"

"No."

"Then chill. Everything will be fine," Troy said, but inside he knew Jake's concern was legitimate. He did like Sadie a lot. He always had. Still, he was a very strong person. When he put his mind to it, he could accomplish anything. He could control himself around Sadie. The simple truth was he didn't have a choice.

Sadie cut through the water one final time and then hoisted herself up the silver ladder. With Troy agree-

ing to keep their deal a secret, she had no compunction
about enjoying her time with his daughters and no
problem enjoying his gorgeous pool.

The way she had this mentoring deal figured, in two
weeks of swimming with the twins—while dressed in
a modest yet attractive swimsuit, thereby proving to
the girls that one didn't have to be seminaked to look
good—and two weeks of casual conversations about
life, she should be able to point them in the right direction. The twins were young. Their ideas couldn't
be so ingrained that Sadie couldn't nudge them out
subtly. And that was all Troy wanted, anyway. He
didn't want her to be obvious, to scold the girls or to
try to change them. He just wanted someone to talk
to them about being a lady and show them a good
example.

Which was fine with Sadie because she wasn't sure
she could do much more than that, since she wasn't
trained to work with children. Being herself, talking
to kids, those were easy. She could handle those. She
could not handle correcting their behavior or disci-
plining them. Those, luckily, were still Troy's job.

She took the final rung on the ladder, stepped onto
the blue and white print ceramic tile that lined the
pool, then faced the two swimming eight-year-olds.
"That's it for me."

The two identical blondes blinked at her. "But we
want to swim!"

"So keep swimming. I'll sit on the pool's edge and
watch you," she said, drying her hair with the fluffy
white towel she had retrieved from a chaise longue.

That seemed to satisfy them, so Sadie lowered herself to the ceramic tile and dipped her feet into the
cool water as she glanced around the opulent estate.

Surrounded by trees, it was naturally secluded, but it also boasted every convenience known to mankind. Shaded benches rimmed twin tennis courts. A pool house provided a place to change and refreshments. A cobblestone path led to a cottagelike guest house.

"This is really heaven," she said, unable to stop the compliment.

Unimpressed, Rosemary ignored the comment, but Ginger looked around as if confused. Obviously accustomed to such luxury, it was clear the little girl couldn't understand what Sadie found so pleasing.

Since she had at least Ginger's attention, Sadie decided there was no time like the present to start chatting and pointing them in the right direction.

"So are you excited to go back to school?"

Ginger and Rosemary exchanged a glance.

"Not really," Ginger said.

Sadie swirled her toe in the water. "Why not?"

"Dad's making us go to Briarhills again," Rosemary said through a long-suffering sigh.

"A private school?"

They nodded.

"We hate it," Ginger said.

Ah. This could explain the progressively bad behavior Troy had described to her father. School opened in three weeks. If they didn't want to go, the closer it got to the first day of school the worse their behavior would be. "You don't like school?"

"We don't like Briarhills," Ginger said.

"It sucks," Rosemary seconded.

"Rosemary!" Sadie said with a gasp, surprised by the little girl's language. "That's not nice."

Clearly confused, Ginger said, "Well, Briarhills does suck."

"I'm not talking about disliking the school!" Sadie said, aghast that the word seemed to be part of her everyday vocabulary. "I'm talking about saying 'suck.' I know it's trendy, maybe even cool, but it's not appropriate for an eight-year-old."

Rosemary sighed as if put upon. "Everybody says sucks."

"Well, it's still not appropriate," Sadie said, cringing when she realized she had slipped from chatting and guiding into discipline, but she knew she couldn't let this slide. Unfortunately, she also knew this wasn't the kind of conversation a person had through a third party, which meant she would have to talk to Troy, after all. But it wouldn't be a long conversation. She would simply advise him of the word Rosemary had used and suggest he discuss it with her.

"So tell me more about private school. Where is it?"

"Philly."

"What?"

"Philadelphia," Ginger said, enunciating every syllable as if Sadie were stupid.

Ginger's attitude rubbed Sadie the wrong way, but again she wasn't here to discipline. Only guide. Set an example. Point them in the right direction. After ten minutes of swimming and two minutes of talking, Sadie couldn't expect them to have picked up any of her cues yet. "You live there?"

"No. We fly there."

Sadie gaped at her. "Every morning?"

Ginger looked at her as if she were crazy. "It's an hour."

"But the drive to and from the airports…"

"We have a private strip, and so does the school."

Rosemary sighed with disgust. "So it only takes us the flight time."

"But you're in a plane every day!"

Ginger rolled her eyes. "Hello! Ever heard of the helicopter?"

Deciding Ginger's attitude wasn't going to shift even if she watched Sadie's ladylike behavior for a hundred years, Sadie put it on her mental list of things to discuss—briefly—with Troy. "You ride a helicopter every day?"

"And wear the freaking ugliest uniforms on the face of the earth."

Freaking went on her mental list of things to discuss with Troy. "They can't be that bad."

"The hell they can't."

All right, all language in general went on the list. Worse, because the twins were so casual with some unsavory words and because their attitude never wavered, Sadie realized Troy had to know about both. He was either deluding himself, believing that having his daughters watch Sadie's good example for two weeks could straighten this out, or he had lied to her and expected her to do a heck of a lot more than what he told her.

The thought that he had tricked her infuriated her, and she hoisted herself from the rim of the pool and headed for the chaise longue to get her cover-up. "You know what? I think I'm going to go talk to your dad."

"You can't," Rosemary said. "You have to watch us. We're not allowed in the pool by ourselves."

"Oh."

Ginger interrupted her. "Never mind. You go ahead. Joe will watch us."

Sadie glanced around. "Who's Joe?"

"The gardener," Rosemary said, then yelled, "Joe!"

A man dressed in cutoff jeans and a tank top appeared from behind the bushes. Though he held pruning shears, he also wore a belt like the one Sadie had seen on Bruce, the cook-bodyguard-driver. Clearly displayed were a phone, pager, two-way radio and a gun.

Another bodyguard.

The man said, "Yeah, half-pint. What's up?"

"Sadie needs to go see Dad," Rosemary said in a very adult tone. "We need a lifeguard."

"I'm your guy," Joe said, strolling over to the pool. When he reached Sadie, he extended his hand to shake hers. "Hi. I'm Joe Montelli. Gardener."

Sadie glanced at his belt then looked him in the eye. "I'm Sadie. I'm...the girls'..." She paused and glanced at the twins in the pool, her heartstrings tugged by unexpected sadness. These girls might have every convenience on the face of the earth, but they were two kids that any teacher, any classmate, anybody who came into contact with them would dislike if only because they had never been disciplined to treat other people with respect. As far as Sadie was concerned, there was no greater misery on the face of the earth than being disliked for something you didn't know you were doing. And no excuse for their father letting them behave like this. They didn't need lessons on how to be a woman, they needed life lessons, lessons Troy should be teaching them, and Sadie was about to tell the illustrious Troy Cramer he shouldn't pawn off his responsibilities but should be handling this problem himself.

When she brought her gaze to Joe's she said, "Friend. I'm the girls' friend." Because by God it was starting to feel like they needed one. They needed somebody not dependent upon their father for a job, because clearly no one else had guts enough to tell Troy the truth.

"I need to talk to you," Sadie said, barreling into Troy's office. He looked up from his computer screen and saw her standing in front of him wearing the white terry-cloth cover-up, but his mind's eye went right past the cover-up and took him directly to the black bathing suit.

And he knew Jake was right. He wasn't going to be able to control his attraction to Sadie as easily as he ignored the attraction he felt to other women.

But Jake was also wrong in thinking Troy couldn't use Sadie's dislike for him to keep himself in line. She didn't like him pushing his weight around. She clearly didn't like anyone telling her what to do. If he continued to push his weight around and tell her what to do, she would continue to be spitting mad, and as long as he never ran into her when she was wearing her gun, neither of them would have anything to worry about.

He flipped off the connection to his secretary in California and as calmly and neutrally as possible he said, "Aren't you supposed to be talking to me through Bruce?"

"We have a problem too big to communicate through other people. Have you talked with your daughters lately?"

"Yes. That's why I hired you," he began, but his phone rang. "Sorry about this. It's the direct line with my accountant so I have to take it." He grabbed the

receiver and said, "Troy Cramer speaking. Hey, Jim.
How's that new baby?" He laughed. "That's great."
He paused. "No, things here are wonderful. Couldn't
be better. Moving the company to Wilburn was the
best decision I ever made." He paused again. "Most
of the staff is transferring..."

He went on, but Sadie tuned him out. Not because
she didn't want to eavesdrop, but because she was
having odd, conflicting feelings. First, he looked great.
Seated behind his big desk, he looked smart, capable,
strong and powerful. Sexy. Commanding. Add that to
his blue eyes and boyish sandy brown hair, and he
was attractive in a way that sneaked up on Sadie and
caused her to react before she thought.

But more than that, though he treated *her* coolly, on
the phone with his friend he sounded like the guy she
remembered from high school. Carefree. Funny. Good
with people. She didn't want to be reminded that he
had been nice. He wasn't nice. He bribed her father
and forced her to work for him. Nice guys didn't bribe
people. Plus, a nice guy would be a better father than
Troy was.

"Sorry about that," he said when he finally got off
the phone. "But the truth is you're going to have to
talk fast because I don't have time..."

As if to prove his statement, Jake Malloy walked
into the room. "Troy, I—" Seeing Sadie, he stopped.
"Oh, hi, Sadie!"

"Hey, Jake," she said and accepted his quick hug.

"I'm so glad you're here. Troy tells me you're helping with the girls."

"I am. I'm—"

"Great," he said, interrupting her. "We're all glad
you took the assignment. And I already told Troy I

would keep your being here a secret. But I need a minute of the boss's time," he added, then promptly usurped ten minutes.

With every second that ticked off the clock, Sadie became angrier. Though the pace of Troy's typical workday explained why he didn't have time to discipline his twins, and Jake's minute-turned-ten proved that Troy and his staff had no concept of time, neither excused Troy. He was a father. He had responsibilities. He couldn't go on ignoring his daughters simply because he was so busy he didn't realize he was ignoring them.

Neither Troy nor Jake noticed when she walked out the door, which didn't merely confirm her conclusions, it fueled the fire of her anger. She could picture Troy's daughters sitting patiently, waiting for their dad until they tired of the stuffy office and left, as Sadie had done. She could see their conversations being interrupted. She could see that they never got a chance to share their dreams, express their fears or even say hello to their dad some days.

And the thought that those sweet little girls were being ignored and then blamed for being bad made Sadie's blood boil. If she had to come back at midnight to catch him when he wasn't busy, Troy Cramer was going to listen to her.

Chapter Three

It wasn't midnight, but stars were twinkling overhead by the time Sadie headed out of town on her way to Troy Cramer's estate. Two emergencies had tacked an extra hour onto her shift, so she couldn't go home to change out of her grimy uniform. But that wasn't the worst of it. She was speeding out of town at eleven o'clock at night, and anyone who saw her would wonder why. Particularly since she wasn't in a police cruiser, but driving her own car, clearly marking her mission as personal. If anyone saw her driving down the lane to Troy's mansion, her career in this town would be over. No one would take her seriously as a police officer and she would probably have to return to Pittsburgh.

But the girls needed her. During her shift she had really thought this situation through, remembering details of everything she had seen in her few hours at Troy's house, and she had come to the conclusion that the twins' problem was threefold. First, they had too much stuff and too much power. The way they reacted to Sadie's appreciation of the estate and then simply ordered Joe to be their lifeguard proved that. Second, Sadie had not seen a woman on the estate, which meant Troy's little girls were being raised in a land of men. *That* explained their vocabulary and their attitudes. Third, their dad was too busy to notice any of it.

When she reached the main gate of the estate, she hit the hidden buzzer and Bruce said, "Yeah, who is it?"

"Bruce, it's me, Sadie. I need to speak with Mr. Cramer."

"Does he know you're coming?"

"He will once you tell him."

"Ouch. I hear that tone." Even as he said it, the big gate began to slide open.

It took a full two minutes to navigate the long lane, and by the time she pulled up to the house, Troy was standing outside the elaborate stained-glass front door waiting for her.

Obviously concerned by her late-night visit, he said, "What's up?"

"I told you this morning," Sadie said as he motioned for her to enter the foyer. "You and I need to talk."

"About the girls?"

"Yes."

"But we made a deal that we would communicate through Bruce."

"I discovered some things today that I need to tell you directly. I told you that this morning, but you got so busy I'm sure you forgot."

He hadn't forgotten. He was hoping that having got-

ten bored waiting, she would take her questions to
Bruce. Not because Troy didn't want to handle them,
but because he couldn't seem to adequately control his
reactions to her. Even now, his heart did a little leap
seeing how cute she was in her police uniform. Talking through Bruce still seemed like the smart way to
handle this. And if he had to keep up the appearance
of being unapproachable to get her to talk to him
through Bruce, then that was what he had to do.

"I'm sorry about all the interruptions, but that's
how my days are."

"Don't sound so proud that everybody and his
brother needs your time and attention. Your busy days
and constant interruptions are the reason your daughters misbehave."

That made him laugh. Working from home, he was
with his girls twenty-four hours a day, seven days a
week. He wasn't going to let her get away with insin-
uating the twins were deprived. Particularly since he
was guessing she felt this way because he had ignored
her. "So you think my daughters misbehave because
I'm busy?"

"Your daughters misbehave because they don't get
enough attention, and the attention they do get is all
wrong!" When her angry words echoed around her in
the empty foyer, she glanced at the cathedral ceiling.
"Could we go somewhere private?"

"Private as in my office, or could we just relax by
the pool?"

Head high, Sadie said, "Pool is fine," and pro-
ceeded to lead him there.

The sliding glass door hadn't fully closed behind
them before she turned on Troy. Seeing the fire in her
green eyes, he knew she meant business.

She gestured to the second-floor windows. "Can the kids hear us?"

"All the rooms have soundproof glass."

"Figures. How about Bruce?"

"He's in his room."

"How can he be in his room? He got the gate."

"He has a monitor in his room."

"Which means he works twenty-four hours a day."

"It's his job. It's also how he wants it. And it's also not something that's going to change," Troy said, getting a little defensive because she was treading on sacred ground. "If you're mad because you don't think I treat Bruce well, then you can turn around and leave. My arrangement with Bruce isn't open to discussion."

Sadie tossed her hands in exasperation. "I don't give a hoot if your deal with Bruce requires he hand over his firstborn male child. But I do care that you're raising two little girls in a land of men!"

He was expecting to be taken to task for being busy. Her comment caught him completely off guard. "What?"

"Look around you, Troy. There isn't a woman for two miles. You have a man who cooks, a male gardener and your business partner is a man. The people I saw shuffling around cleaning are men. You don't even have a secretary, but if you did I would bet it would be a guy."

Troy smiled crookedly. "You have something against men?"

"Troy! You have two little girls. Two *girls*. They're not sassy because they're bad. They're sassy because that's the kind of conversation they hear you and your friends have. They aren't bossy because they're spoiled. They're bossy because *you* are the boss, and by association so are they. Ginger and Rosemary routinely tell Joe and Bruce, two two-hundred-and-fifty-pound men, what to do, and they jump to do it. How can you be surprised that they don't behave normally?''

Seeing her point but confounded by it, Troy sat on one of the chaise longues. "I don't know."

"Why did you set this up this way?"

He glanced at her. When she first arrived he noticed she looked very cute in her police uniform. Right now, all he saw was the fire in her eyes and her gun. Not that he thought she would shoot him, but it just seemed ridiculous to be arguing with a woman who was armed. Particularly since he had been going out of his way to make her stay mad at him.

"I didn't set it up this way. It just sort of happened. When I hired these guys, I wasn't really thinking about household staff, per se. I was looking for ways to subtly integrate bodyguards.''

"And you couldn't subtly integrate a female?"

"I've integrated you—''

"I'm temporary!" Frustrated, she paced away. When he didn't say anything for several seconds, she faced him. "Why are you staring at me?"

"Could we put the gun on the table?"

"No."

"Please? You seem a little mad, and I don't want to tempt fate.''

"I'm not going to shoot you!" Sadie said, clearly exasperated. "Though part of me wonders if you don't deserve it. For Pete's sake, Troy, how could you not notice you have no women around here?''

"Probably because there *are* women in my day. The majority of my office staff is women, and I routinely video conference with them. My secretary, who works in California, is a woman. She's on-screen beside me almost all eight hours of her workday. The only time she's not with me is when I shut her off to make phone calls or hold meetings, the way a normal boss would close the door." He paused to take a breath, then added, "I never noticed there were no women around the house because there are plenty of women in my day. And I'd still feel more comfortable if you would put the gun on the table."

Sadie sighed. "Modern technology."

"Don't knock it. It paid for everything you see around you."

"Right. It's also caused you to miss something fundamental in raising your girls."

"Not really," Troy said, realizing that by keeping her angry with him he had probably made himself look stupid to her. And he wasn't. He might not know everything about raising children. But he wanted to learn. He wanted good daughters and he wanted to be a good dad. That was why he had brought Sadie to his house in the first place.

"I knew something was wrong, so I hired you. I might have been off base about what needed to be done to fix things, but I wasn't completely oblivious."

"Right."

"Don't say 'right' as if you think I'm an idiot. That doesn't help any of us. Give me some suggestions for how to get things back on track."

"All right," Sadie said, then rotated her head and shoulders.

"Sore neck?"

"Yeah. It was a long night. There were two accidents on my shift."

Guilt stabbed at Troy. Because of him she was working two jobs, and from the look of her she was exhausted. Worse, she had driven to his house because he had ignored her when she tried to talk to him. All because he couldn't control his attraction to her.

"I'm sorry. I didn't think through that working for me would mean you had two jobs."

Sadie shrugged. "It's not that big a deal."

It was to Troy. Technically, she was here tonight, after a long shift, because he had been running scared. And that was just stupid. He was a grown man who had never had a problem controlling himself. If he put his mind to it, he could do just about anything. That meant he could ignore a few sexual responses. He had to start behaving like his normal self, the way he did with the rest of his staff, or Sadie would think he was disinterested in his daughters or a mean-spirited old goat, too grouchy to raise two little girls.

He scooted back on the chaise, arranged his legs on either side to make room for her to sit in front of him and patted the cushion. "Come here. I give a great back rub."

That made her laugh. "I'm sure."

"I do! Staring at a computer all day is high-tension work. Everybody gets a sore neck. In the California office there is a masseuse on staff. He taught me a few tricks so when the going got tough I could step in and help him."

She peeked at him. "No kidding."

He smiled, glad that he had come to his senses and she was responding. He couldn't have a relationship with her, but that didn't mean they couldn't be friends. And his back rubs, like her study halls, were legendary.

"No kidding. Come on. Let me rub your shoulders."

She sighed.

"I'm harmless."

"I'll bet."

"Really. You hate me. You hate my money. I would have to be an idiot to try something knowing you'd shoot me down...or just plain shoot me," he said, chuckling and nodding at her gun. "You're perfectly safe."

He recognized she agreed when she cautiously made her way to the chaise. She sat, but eased back only as far as she had to.

Troy dropped his fingers to her shoulders. Getting her accustomed to having his hands on her, he kneaded gently for a few seconds, then slid his palms down her arms. The skin left bare by the short sleeves of her uniform shirt felt like pure velvet, but he ignored the sensations that ricocheted through him, first because he needed to mend his reputation with her, but also because he was a gentleman. As long as he remembered that, he was sure he would be fine.

Coolly detached, he eased his fingers along her tense neck muscles, loosening them with the techniques he had learned from Eduardo. "Now, let's get back to the twins. You were going to give me suggestions for how to fix the mess I seem to have made of their lives."

"Are you really going to listen to my suggestions?"

"I love suggestions."

"Good, because..." She stopped when Troy squeezed the muscle linking her neck and shoulder. "Oh, gosh, that feels good."

She sighed with pleasure, and Troy shifted closer,

pleased that with a little determination he could control himself and begin to ease them toward a normal association. Having her seated between his legs packed the situation with sensual possibilities, but he knew none of them would happen—couldn't happen, too much was riding on this relationship remaining platonic—so he steeled himself against the persistent reactions his body insisted on having. He focused instead on making her relax so she would tell him the truth, so they could have a fruitful discussion about his daughters, because that was how he worked. He hired experts, then he trusted them.

"Go on about the twins," he urged.

"Well, today they talked about school and they not only explained that they fly there every day in a helicopter, but also they told me school sucked."

He frowned. "The girls dislike school?"

She turned enough that she could gape at him. "Whether or not they like school isn't the issue."

Troy stopped massaging. "It's not?"

"No. It's not. The problem is that they routinely use words that aren't appropriate for little girls."

He knew that, of course, but to him, the vocabulary itself didn't seem as important as the girls' hating school. "You're not concerned that they don't like school?"

"Yes!" she said, turning to present her back to him again so he could continue to rub her shoulders. "But that comes under a different heading. Their vocabulary is priority number one, because if we don't change that, it won't matter if they don't like school. School won't like them."

"Sorry. You're right. I'll talk to them."

"I don't want you to talk to them. I want you to talk to Jake, Joe and Bruce."

"What do they have to do with anything?" Troy asked as he ran his fingers down the bumps of her spine. Instead of her tension decreasing, it seemed to be compounding. And that wouldn't do. He could blame her lack of response on their discussion, but he knew he wasn't giving his best massage. "This works better if I'm not rubbing through material."

She turned and gaped at him. "Don't even think I'm taking off my shirt."

"Not off, just out. Untuck it from your police pants."

She gaped at him. "Not on your life!"

"Look, you don't like me and you have a gun. You couldn't be safer. So explain to me why you think Jake, Joe and Bruce are such a threat."

She sighed, yanked her shirt from her trousers and faced forward. "I don't know about Joe and Bruce, but I know Jake. He's one of my brother's best friends, so I know how he talks. I'm betting it's his language more than anyone else's that they copy."

Troy slid his hands beneath her loose cotton shirt. "Jake's language can get a tad salty," he said as he nonchalantly kneaded her supple skin. Sensation after sensation buffeted him. Lusty visions knocked at the door of his mind. Considering her gun and his pride at how controlled he could be with her, he ordered the invading thoughts to go away.

She sighed brokenly. "That feels so good. I wish I had those hands waiting for me at the end of every shift."

He did, too. He really did. The visions knocked

again, but he sent a mental guard dog to the imaginary
door of his mind and kept kneading.

"I know Jake's language isn't the best," he said.
"But I've never actually heard him swear in front of
the girls."

"I'm guessing he doesn't, but that the girls hear him
when they are walking up the hall to visit you or when
he's on his way to the kitchen and totally unaware that
the girls are around."

Realizing how easily that could happen, Troy nodded. "Right. I never thought of that."

"Imagine what the girls' headmistress will think if
the girls find a way or reason to tell her her school
sucks."

"They'll be out on their ears," Troy said, picking
up on something else she was saying. "The girls' language is only the tip of the iceberg, isn't it?"

She peeked at him over her shoulder. "Sorry."

"So what else do I need to do?"

"First, like I said before, you should get a woman
in here somewhere."

Slowly, methodically, Troy continued to work his
fingers up her back, unexpectedly struck by a streak
of stubborn possessiveness. As far as he was concerned, he already had a woman in his daughters'
lives. Sadie. Unfortunately, he also knew he wasn't
going to keep her. But right now he wanted to. He
really, really wanted to. If she married him, he would
get to touch her skin anytime he wanted....

He stopped his thoughts. Right then. Right there.
How could he be thinking about marrying her? That
was ridiculous! He hardly knew her. What he was reacting to were the feelings and sensations touching her
aroused in him. So he had to stop having reactions.

He had to mentally tie up and gag the lusty thoughts that sprang to life every time he noticed that her skin felt like velvet or that her muscles quivered with his every touch.

He ignored the tremors shivering through her flesh by paying attention to the suggestions she was making about the kind of woman who would fit with the girls and the jobs he could create to bring one into his household. Out of necessity, he became so engrossed in the discussion that he forgot all about the back of her bra. When he bumped it, it broke his concentration. Crisp lace skimmed his fingertips, then his palms.

A tidal wave of sensation washed through him, shocking him so much that the lusty thoughts broke their bindings and burst through the door of his mind. Every red-blooded American cell in his body bounced to life.

"Getting a woman in here shouldn't be too hard," he said, but the words came out in a croak. He scooted away from her, wisely putting lots of space between them. "My human resources director is a woman. She's the first person coming from California. She'll be working here at the house until we find a building."

Blissfully unaware, Sadie scooted back, too, negating the space, allowing him easy access to continue her massage. "Great," she said, happy with his answer, and also obviously relaxed and completely ignorant of Troy's dilemma.

Which was good, because he didn't want to have to explain himself. But also bad, because, perversely, it annoyed him that she wasn't having any kind of sexual reaction. No, it insulted him. He wasn't a bad-looking guy. She had said so herself.

He told himself to stop caring and stop even think-

ing about being attracted to her and wanting her to be
attracted to him. He took a slow, measured breath and
tried to move back again but encountered the thick
cushion of the chaise.

"What else should we do for the girls?" he asked,
desperate to get his mind off the fact that he was rubbing her back and she was between his legs.

"Troy, there are a million things we need to talk
about tonight. We're probably going to be here until
two o'clock discussing this. But before we get into the
tough stuff about *your* end of the deal, do you understand about having a chat with Jake, Joe and Bruce?"

Good. Jake, Joe and Bruce were good. Three un-
appealing men were exactly what Troy needed to think
about to cool his libido.

"Yes. I will talk with Jake, Joe and Bruce about
their language," Troy said, taking more slow, measured breaths to cool himself down. And it was working. Because he was an honest, decent guy, raising two
daughters, and he didn't fool around with sex god-
desses. Well, maybe he would if he were in a better
position....

Position. Damn it. Did he have to think of that par-
ticular word? Where the hell was his mind?

Actually, it was on the skin beneath his palm, the
very smooth, very feminine skin he was rubbing into
a mass of very soft, very relaxed muscle.

"That does feel wonderful."

"Yes, it does." Oh, great! He'd said that out loud.
She turned, a puzzled expression on her face.

Yep, he'd said it out loud, and there wasn't a
damned thing he could say to get himself out of this.
Nothing. If she scooted back a fraction of an inch, she
would know exactly why he had said what he had said.

Troy didn't move a muscle, but as he stared at her he couldn't help but notice how pretty her face was. Smooth, creamy skin created soft, feminine lines. Her black hair brought out the color of her bright green eyes. And then there was her mouth. Wide and shapely, formed by very pink, very kissable lips.

He felt himself being drawn forward, and the night sounds around him fell away. Even the lusty thoughts in his head went perfectly still, waiting, it seemed, to see what would happen next so they would know which direction to take.

With his gaze locked with Sadie's, he moved closer until, in the last second, he watched her eyelids drop. Permission, Troy believed, that he could kiss her.

So he did. He negated the last fraction of an inch between them and touched his mouth to hers.

Her lips were soft and warm. Inviting, tempting, tantalizing. They were sweet enough that he could have kept going, deepened the kiss and never looked back. But the lightning bolt of arousal that thundered through his body was hot enough to stop him cold.

He had promised her she was safe with him! He didn't want another woman in his life, and she certainly didn't need him in hers. Yet, like a lovesick schoolboy he had kissed her.

He pulled away quickly and bounced off the chaise. "That will never happen again."

Sadie also jumped up. But where Troy was dumbfounded, she appeared to be furious. "No, it won't!"

Confused by his loss of control and once again offended that she didn't seem to find him attractive, Troy said, "I got your point this morning. You don't want to be involved with me. I get it. You don't have to be insulting about it."

"If you get it then you wouldn't have kissed me." She paced away, combing her fingers through her thick hair, which glowed in the moonlight. "You're a rich man with an ego the size of Ohio who thinks money buys everything. You're the last person on the face of the earth I want to kiss."

"Yeah, well, you're a prickly woman who carries a gun. All you've done since I ran into you yesterday is yell at me or complain. If you think anything but impulse caused me to kiss you, you're crazy!"

Just as Troy said that, Bruce opened the French door. From the look on his face he hadn't heard any part of their discussion. Troy was glad for the sound-proof glass.

"I'm sorry to interrupt you, boss. But you have a call."

"Thanks, Bruce," Troy said, walking toward the door without a backward glance at Sadie. "Show Ms. Evans out."

Chapter Four

When Sadie arrived at her parents' house, it was quiet. Though she immediately crawled into the twin bed in the room she was sharing with Hannah until she got her own apartment, Sadie stayed awake half the night trying to understand why Troy kissing her had had such an effect on her.

When his lips touched her, she could have easily fainted, the electricity between them was so hot. But that didn't make any sense. She didn't *want* to like him. He wasn't a very nice person. Plus she had a mission. She had started working for him to earn money for Aunt Sadie, but she now realized those poor little girls really needed her. And she took that seriously. She couldn't believe one stupid kiss could distract her.

She fell asleep angry with herself, and the next thing she knew it was morning. By the time she got downstairs the coffee her parents had made for breakfast was too stale to drink. With no time to make a fresh pot before she left for her scheduled swim with Troy's girls, Sadie stopped at the diner to grab her daily fix of caffeine.

"Hey, Charlotte!"

"Hey, there, Sadie Belle. What can I get for you?"

"Just coffee. And to go. I'm already late for an appointment."

Charlotte's two perfectly drawn red-brown eyebrows waggled. "Is that what they're calling it nowadays? An appointment?"

"I've always called appointments appointments."

Charlotte laughed. "You used to call them dates."

"Ha!" This time Sadie laughed. "I haven't had a date since I moved home."

"Okay, whatever," Charlotte said, handing Sadie the disposable cup full of coffee. "If you don't want the world to know you're dating Troy Cramer, I'm not going to be the one to spill the beans."

"Charlotte!" Sadie said desperately as she glanced around in dismay, realizing everybody in the diner was within hearing distance of that comment. "I'm not dating Troy Cramer!"

"Right. You went out to his estate at eleven o'clock last night to get investment advice."

"Or," George McDougal called from his spot three stools down the counter, "she needed help with her computer."

Everybody laughed.

"I'm not dating him!"

"Right! That's why your car was seen pulling into his driveway. That's why the gates opened for you when nobody else can get in. Because you're *not* dating him."

"I'm not! I'm helping him with his daughters."

Everybody laughed again.

"Uh-huh," George said. "Troy didn't pick Hannah or Caro, two teachers, to help his kids. He picked you, the local policewoman. We're buying that one, Sadie."

"Hey! *I'm* good with kids!"

"Right!"

"I am!"

"We don't dispute that you might be good with kids," Charlotte said. "It's just that if you wanted to keep it a secret that you were dating the richest guy in town, you should have come up with a better excuse to be at his house than being needed by two little girls who probably have everything they want at their fingertips."

Everybody laughed again, and righteous indignation rose up in Sadie. But she wasn't upset because of the teasing. She was angry because absolutely no one understood Troy Cramer's twins or their lives. Everybody was so certain Troy's girls had the perfect life that no one saw their misery.

No one except Sadie and, by God, if it killed her she was going to help them.

Suddenly, she didn't give a damn what one person in this diner—in this town—thought of her. Especially if it got in the way of helping Ginger and Rosemary.

She took her change from Charlotte's hand and turned toward the diner door. "George, you need a job. Charlotte, you need a life. And the rest of you probably have high cholesterol from all the butter Artie puts on the toast. Before you go butting your noses into everybody else's affairs, I would think you should solve your own problems."

With her head high and for the first time free of

giving a damn what everybody thought, she walked out of the diner and into the morning sun, as angry with Troy Cramer as she was with the people of Wilburn. Not only were those sad little girls his responsibility, but also he'd promised her she was perfectly safe with him. Then he went and kissed her.

There were only two possible reasons for that. Either he lied, and she wasn't safe with him. Or he kissed her for a reason that had nothing to do with liking her. When she took all the emotion out of what had happened between them the night before, the bottom line was that their discussion had ended because he had kissed her. And when she looked at it completely objectively, she realized he might have kissed her to end the discussion.

The more she thought about it, the more it infuriated her. Not so much because of the embarrassment at how the kiss affected her, though there was that, but more because it was very selfish of him to end the conversation because he was afraid she might say something he didn't want to hear, something that would force him to reevaluate his life. His daughters needed him. *Him.* He had to face the fact that his life had to change. And the way she felt this morning, Sadie was exactly the person to make him change it.

Knowing she and Troy were about to have a showdown, she marched up the walk to the front door ready for a confrontation. But when she let herself into the foyer, the house felt oddly empty. The corridor that led to the wing of offices was dark. So rather than search for Troy there, she made her way to the kitchen where Bruce was making an apple pie.

"Hey, Bruce. Where's Troy?"

"Mr. Cramer flew to California this morning."

"He what?"

"He flew to California. To the corporate office. It's one of the perks of having a private plane," Bruce said with a laugh. "He comes and goes as he pleases."

"I'll bet he does," Sadie said, keeping the displeasure out of her voice so Bruce wouldn't hear it. Just as she had thought, Troy was avoiding her. He heard as much as he wanted to hear before he cut her off. He had no intention of changing his lifestyle or the way he worked and no intention of giving Sadie another chance to tell him he should. Why? The better question was why should he? He'd said himself that when he couldn't do something he hired someone to do it for him. He probably figured if he stayed away long enough Sadie would fix the girls' problems herself.

She drummed her fingers on the butcher block, absently watching Bruce as he peeled apples. Troy might have thought he had bested her because he had better tools and better toys, but he didn't know the rules of the game had changed since she no longer feared the town would discover she was working for him. That gave her an upper hand he didn't know she had.

Still, before she flew off half-cocked, believing she was right about Troy's not wanting to change his life, Sadie decided to give him one more opportunity to redeem himself. One question properly answered by Bruce would save him.

She stole a bite of apple from the batch Bruce had soaking in salt water and casually asked the burly bodyguard, "Did he happen to talk to you before he left?"

"Sure, he reminded me of the three hundred and

forty-seven household tasks he expects me to oversee, then flew out the door.''

''He didn't say anything about the girls?''

Bruce thought a second then said, ''Nothing except that if either of them accidentally puts a boa in the wash I'm supposed to toss it in the trash.''

''He didn't say anything about watching your language around the girls?''

Bruce blanched. ''No.''

''I see.''

''Am I doing something wrong?''

Completely disappointed in Troy Cramer, Sadie shook her head. He hadn't even done the one thing he had promised he would do—talk to his staff.

''The girls' language yesterday morning was a little off. They use some slang that's inappropriate. I asked Troy to talk with you, Jake Malloy, Joe the gardener and all the cleaning people to make sure you consider your words carefully even when the twins aren't in the room, because you never know when they are just around the corner.''

Wide-eyed with contrition, Bruce said, ''Absolutely.''

''Good,'' Sadie said, glancing around. ''By the way, where are the girls?''

''Upstairs. Are you going to swim?''

''Nope. I'm taking them on a field trip.''

''A field trip?''

''Don't panic. I'm just taking them to my aunt's day care.''

''I don't think…''

''This isn't your call. It's mine. The way you guys talk isn't the only thing that's screwing up those two sweet kids. Being around only adults isn't good for them, either. So today they're going to associate with kids their own age."

"But Troy never..."

"Precisely," Sadie said, cleverly misinterpreting him to stop his argument. "That's why I'm going to."

Bruce's hands flew to his apron strings. He quickly untied them and pulled the thing over his head. "I have to go with you."

"You can't."

He tossed the apron to the counter and put a lid on the container of peeled apples. "I have to. Ms. Evans, whether you know it or not, *this,* protecting the girls, is my job. It's disguised, and I do it low-key. But my main function is to keep them safe. You won't stop me. And if you do, no matter how good you are with those girls, you will be fired."

His careful enunciation of the last four words caused them to sink in exactly as he wanted them to, and Sadie knew when she was beat. Yesterday she would have been happy to be fired. Today she knew she couldn't leave until things changed for Troy's daughters. In fact, today she knew she might have to be the person who changed things around here. And if that meant she had to compromise, then she would compromise. "Okay. How good a Wiffle ball player are you?"

"How safe is this day care?"

"There's a six-foot fence around the backyard and trees that surround the fence. The gate is locked, and no one gets onto the property without being buzzed in. It's sort of like the front gate to this estate, but a little different."

He flexed his bicep. "Then I'm an exceptional Wiffle ball player."

She looked at his muscles and laughed. "Don't count on it. Your strength will work against you since it's an airy plastic ball."

He caught her gaze and held it. "I know when to use my muscles and when to lay back."

"Then you will fit in beautifully."

The girls, dressed in denim shorts and T-shirts, happily ran down the elegant spiral staircase and headed for the front door. Sadie stopped them in the foyer, turned them around and pointed them in the direction of their rooms to scrub off their makeup.

"But I want—" Ginger began.

Sadie interrupted her. "You're about to meet my mother. She doesn't like it when women, even fashion models, even women on TV, even circus clowns, wear too much makeup."

"But—"

"She's very into natural beauty," Sadie said, and Bruce expertly picked up the ball.

"And you two are the prettiest. Why not show Miss Sadie's mom how pretty you are?"

That seemed to snag Rosemary's interest, and she nodded and dashed up the steps. With a heavy sigh Ginger followed her. When they returned, they looked like eight-year-old girls with freshly scrubbed faces.

"Ready to play Wiffle ball?" Sadie asked as Bruce herded the girls into the SUV.

"What's Wiffle ball?" Ginger asked.

"It's like baseball but with a plastic ball that looks like Swiss cheese. And it requires a lot of skill and agility rather than strength."

"Sounds lame," Ginger said, sighing as she glanced out the car window.

Rosemary looked at her for a second, then decided to agree. "Yeah, lame."

"You know, the two of you are allowed to think for yourselves."

"We do think for ourselves."

"No, you don't. You copy each other." Sadie turned in the seat to face the girls as Bruce drove them to town. "Rosemary wanted to take off the makeup. Ginger, you didn't. Yet you went upstairs and did it anyway."

"You would have been mad if I didn't."

"Yeah, but you didn't look to me for advice, you looked to Rosemary." She paused and glanced at the other twin. "And Rosemary, you might like Wiffle ball, but you didn't even wait to see what the game was like, you simply took your sister's opinion." She shifted to face front again. "You two have got to learn to think for yourselves."

The girls were quiet for the rest of the trip, apparently mulling over her advice. When they reached town, Sadie directed Bruce to the day care, and he pulled the SUV to the small parking lot just outside the gate, then helped the girls out of the vehicle.

"Do you do that all the time?" Sadie asked.

"What?"

"Virtually carry them around. If anything's even the slightest bit hard, like the little jump that would be required to get out of the SUV, you do it for them."

"It's my job."

Sadie said only, "Hmm," as she guided the girls and Bruce to the gate. Her mother answered her request to be let in, then Sadie led her troop up the steps of the porch in the back of the two-story beige house that served as the day care. The second she opened the door the sound of babies crying greeted her. Rosemary grabbed Sadie's right thigh and hung on for dear life. Ginger clung to her left.

"They're babies!" Sadie said with a laugh, pulling the girls into the huge room ringed by toy boxes. "There's nothing to be afraid of."

Ginger glanced at Sadie, her blue eyes huge and frightened. "They're so loud."

"They're probably hungry."

"Or maybe there's a diaper problem," Bruce said, bending to get close to the girls' faces, teasing them.

"Oh, gross!"

They said it in stereo and loud enough for Sadie's father to hear. Dark-haired, green-eyed Pete Evans turned and smiled, then strolled over to greet them.

"Hey, honey," he said, leaning around the twins to hug Sadie. The girls tightened their holds on her legs. "Who do we have here?"

"These are Troy Cramer's twins, Dad. Ginger and Rosemary. And this is Bruce Oliver. He's a friend of the family," she said, sending a message with her eyes so that her dad would understand there was a lot more to the story than she could say in front of the girls.

"Oh," Pete said knowingly, then he turned to Bruce and extended his hand. "How do you do, Mr. Oliver."

"Fine. Thank you. Thank you for having us this morning. I understand we play Wiffle ball here."

"Yes, we do, and you look like you would make a good team captain."

"I'd whip the troops into shape, sir."

Sadie laughed. "Men." She placed her hands on the twins' shoulders and nudged them forward. "Come on. Let's go get a look at the babies."

Rosemary clearly dragged her feet, but Ginger, usually the cranky one, was surprisingly accommodating. About a foot away from the row of changing tables, Sadie paused and let the girls walk forward on their own. Unfortunately, they stopped about six inches away. Ginger stood on tiptoes to get a better look at six-month-old Jack Basil.

"Oh! He's so little," she gasped.

"And isn't baby Jack sweet?" Sadie said, trying to encourage Ginger closer.

But Ginger stood frozen until the baby smiled at her and made a loud singing noise as if he was glad to see her, then she cautiously took the final steps to the table.

"He likes you," Sadie said.

"Hi, Jack," Ginger said, her voice filled with awe when the baby gurgled his reply. She looked at Sadie. "He's so cute!"

"Yes, he is."

"Can I hold him?"

Lilly Evans walked behind Ginger. As usual, Sadie's mom wore her graying blond hair in a tight bun, and her brown eyes sparkled with life. "Well, you could hold Jack, but he's pretty big, and you would have to be very careful, so I have a better idea. Why don't we put him on a blanket on the floor with some toys? Then you could sit beside him and entertain him."

Ginger's eyes grew round with excitement. "Really?"

"Sure." Lilly reached for Jack. "Come on, pumpkin."

The baby squealed with delight. Ginger clapped her hands together with glee, and Sadie's mom led them away.

"What about you, Rosemary? What do you…" Sadie glanced at the second twin and didn't get the rest of her question out of her mouth. Rosemary stood beside the changing table, but she was staring out the window at the group of kids playing in the yard.

"Want to go outside?"

Rosemary faced Bruce and swallowed hard. "Can I?"

Sadie's heart melted. For Pete's sake. These kids were eight years old, but they had to ask permission to play.

"Sure, Rosie." Bruce spoke to Rosemary, but he caught Sadie's gaze, sending her a clear message. "We'll leave Ginger in here with Jack and Sadie," he said, accenting Sadie's name so she would know she was physically responsible for the second twin. "And you and I will go outside."

Bruce led Rosemary out the door and down the steps to the yard, then integrated himself into the game the same way Sadie's father always did. Partly as organizer and referee and partly as the watchdog who didn't let the ball go too far or the game get too rough.

With Ginger busy entertaining Jack with a squeaky toy and out of earshot, Sadie faced her mother. She sighed and said, "Can you believe this?"

"I'm not sure I have a clear picture of what's going on."

"I do. And it took me less than twenty-four hours with the kids to see it."

"They're spoiled?"

"They're deprived! They have everything except a mother figure, friends and real interaction with other people."

Lilly winced. "Ouch. Why don't you tell me how you really feel?"

"It's not funny, Mom. Technically, they have everything."

"But they have nothing."

"It's sad, and the worst of it is, Troy Cramer's so busy providing them with enough money to have every gadget known to mankind that he doesn't even see he's depriving them of normal things, and that's what's making them different."

"I get the impression that's why he hired you. He knows he needs help."

"I plan to give him help, all right."

"Sadie," her mother said, using Sadie's name like a warning.

Sadie sighed. "Relax, Mom, I'm helping him by bringing the girls here." She sighed and glanced around uneasily. "Even though he didn't authorize the trip, and I'm pretty sure he's going to hate it." Sadie shook her head. "But I didn't have a chance to run it by him. Heck, I haven't even really been able to explain his girls' problems to him yet. I tried to talk to him last night, and he wouldn't listen." She paused, not quite sure how to phrase her explanation without telling her mother Troy kissed her. "He…distracted us and then just kind of left. This morning, he was gone, as if he doesn't want to talk about this. Which I'm assuming means he wants me to handle things myself so he doesn't have to. But the more I think about Bruce's reaction to bringing the girls here, the more I realize I'm going to pay for taking the twins off the estate."

"Hm," Lilly said, "that might be a good thing. The minute Troy reprimands you, you have an opening to tell him that you didn't have a choice but to take the girls without his permission, and that if he wants you to help him, he's got to trust you."

"It's not that easy. The problem isn't so much that Troy needs to trust me as much as it is that Troy needs to spend more time with the girls himself."

"Well, that shouldn't be too hard to explain to him."

"It is when Troy thinks he already is involved in their lives."

Lilly frowned. "How can he think he's involved in their lives if he isn't?"

"I haven't talked with him about this, but I'm guessing that because he's home and so are the girls, he thinks they are together. Because he can see them out his office window and is technically in the same house as they are, I think he feels he's with them twenty-four hours a day."

"So what are you going to do?"

Sadie glanced around the day care. "I'm not sure. The bottom line is that he himself is the problem, and I don't think he wants to hear that. I think that's why he...distracted us...last night and why he wasn't at the house this morning."

Lilly nodded thoughtfully. "Just remember what I said about taking advantage of the situation if he's upset with you. You never know when you can turn the tables."

Anticipating a lecture, a reprimand and maybe even a fight to keep the job she hadn't wanted this time yesterday, Sadie was primed and ready for Troy's return late that night. After her shift, she changed out of her uniform and drove to Troy's mansion to find the girls still waiting up for him. When the sound of his little blue sports car pulling up the circular drive rolled through the patio where Sadie and the twins were playing a board game, both girls squealed. All Sadie's muscles tensed, and her blood heated with anger over the way he had twice gotten out of the discussion they needed to have. But he wasn't getting out tonight. She was ready.

"Dad's home!" Ginger cried, running to the French doors and up the corridor to the foyer, Rosemary on her heels. Ever present Bruce was right behind them. Not exactly hanging back, but watchful.

Sadie straightened her shoulders. Bruce had explained the trip to the day care to Troy when he called to check in, and from Bruce's reaction Sadie knew Troy wasn't pleased. The second he stepped in the front door Sadie expected him to say, "Ms. Evans, you and I need to talk." And she was ready to coolly reply, "Yes, we most certainly do."

Now all he needed to do was walk through the door.

Standing in the foyer with the twins, she started the count down in her head—three, two, one—and right on time the door opened.

But Troy Cramer wasn't the person who stepped into the black and gold foyer. The person who walked through the door was Joni Somers, one of Sadie's high school friends, a woman who had sort of disappeared after graduation.

"Hello, girls."

"Joni!" the twins squealed.

"Joni!" Sadie gasped.

"Sadie!" Joni dropped her sleek white leather overnight bag and walked over to grab both of Sadie's hands. "My gosh! It's been ten years."

"Yes, it has," Sadie said, her voice squeaky with confusion. Not only had she been expecting Troy to walk through the door, but also Joni was drop-dead gorgeous. The former chubby girl from high school had gotten taller, thinner and more sophisticated than most women would ever be. Dressed in a black sheath with her blond hair tucked into a perfect chignon, Joni carried herself with the demeanor of a princess.

"You look great."

Joni laughed. "As always, you're the belle of the ball, though."

Troy entered the foyer, grabbed the twins and began a noisy reunion with his daughters. In his black suit, white shirt and blue silk tie, he looked as elegant as Joni. His sandy brown hair was combed to perfection. No wayward strands tumbled sexily to his forehead. His jacket was buttoned. His tie was straight.

Sadie glanced at her jeans and T-shirt. "I'm hardly the belle of the ball this evening."

Joni only laughed. "You could wear sackcloth and be on the cover of *Vogue.* You always could!" She squeezed Sadie's fingers. "It's so wonderful to see you."

"It's great to see you, too, Joni," Sadie said. In the background she heard the twins saying, "Do we have to?" and "Aw!" as Troy calmly reminded them that it was close to midnight and past their bedtimes. Two heavy sighs were followed by sad little voices saying, "Good night, Dad."

"Forgive me for missing a memo or something," Sadie said, smiling awkwardly at Joni. "But what are you doing here?"

"Joni is my director of human resources," Troy said, as the twins headed upstairs. "She's here permanently now. In fact, she'll be living here until she finds her own place. But that's okay since we decided we needed a woman here for the girls anyway, right?''

Sadie's brow furrowed with confusion. The surprises just kept coming. Troy might be downplaying the significance of Joni being here, but if he had flown the whole way to California to speed up Joni's transfer to Wilburn, then he had been listening to her the night before.

He had been listening to her the night before. And, obviously, by bringing Joni to the house he had taken what she said to heart. He did care about his daughters. He wasn't trying to get out of caring for them. He was simply taking her advice one step at a time.

So what had that kiss been all about then?

Troy smiled at Joni, and Joni smiled at him. Sadie's stomach clenched sickly. She had the oddest case of unease about Joni living with Troy.

"I hadn't expected to be moving until next month," Joni said. "But Troy flew to L.A. this morning and made me an offer I couldn't refuse."

Joni smiled at Troy again, and this time full-fledged jealousy rattled through Sadie, shocking her. Darn it! She was not jealous! The last man in the world she wanted was Troy Cramer. He threw his money around to get his own way, didn't spend enough time with his daughters to understand their troubles and was about to reprimand her for taking the twins off the estate. He was not the nice guy Sadie remembered from high school. Bringing Joni into the house as a role model for the girls didn't save him, because if he intended to date Joni, the new relationship might make things worse for Ginger and Rosemary.

Reminded of the girls and her position as their advocate, Sadie asked, "What kind of offer?"

"He doubled my salary."

"How nice," Sadie said. Anger sizzled through her. Once again he was throwing his money around.

"You said the girls needed a woman. I got them one."

Sadie almost said, "What am I? Chopped liver?" but she stopped herself, not quite sure how that had popped into her head.

She took a quick breath and reminded herself she was temporary and intended to stay that way. The girls needed someone permanent in their lives. Joni had changed as much since high school as Sadie had, so she was a good choice. And if Troy wanted to date her, he should be allowed. He had a right to date whomever he wanted.

Sadie straightened her shoulders, forced all the odd thoughts of jealousy out of her head and smiled brightly. "Well, then, I guess I'll just be on my way so you can get settled in."

She started for the door, but Troy caught her arm. "Oh, no, you don't. You and I need to talk."

Chapter Five

Leading Troy down the hall to his office, Sadie felt very much like she was on her way to her execution, but she held her head high and shoved her shoulders back. She was a policewoman, for Pete's sake. A computer nerd could not intimidate her.

She had herself convinced of that until Troy closed the door behind them and faced her. Even standing in front of the bank of computers positioned along the back wall of his den, Troy Cramer looked quite the opposite of a computer nerd. In his suit jacket, with his tie loose, he looked incredibly sexy.

"What in the hell did you think you were doing, taking the girls out without my permission?" he asked angrily.

"My job!" Sadie countered, remembering her position as the girls' advocate and forcing herself to forget about the ridiculous physical attraction she felt for their father.

"Your job," he said, striding past her and around

his desk, "is to set a good enough example that they stop wearing an inch and a half of makeup, feather boas and hip huggers!"

"And did you notice what they had on tonight?"

Obviously primed to issue an angry retort, Troy froze by his tall-backed burgundy leather chair. His face twisted with confusion as he said, "T-shirts. Jean shorts."

"And not a drop of makeup."

He sat on the chair. "Yeah."

"And they didn't miss any of it."

He peered across the desk at her. "They didn't?"

"No! And do you know why?"

He impatiently motioned for Sadie to take a seat. "Sadie, we could go on like this all night," he said, clearly frustrated with her. "Or you could just spit out whatever it is you want to say."

"All right, they didn't miss the makeup because they were doing kid things all day. Bruce and I took them to the day care around eight. Rosemary played Wiffle ball all morning."

"No kidding?"

"No kidding. And Ginger was mother's helper with the babies."

"What's mother's helper?"

"Someone who hangs around my mother all morning and gets blankets and diapers and holds the bottle while my mother burps the babies."

As Sadie spoke, Troy's expression softened. It went from angry to surprised to almost joyful. "Ginger likes babies?"

"Adores them."

"Her mother did, too."

At the mention of the twins' mother, Sadie stiffened. Not because she didn't want to hear, but because she realized she did.

Slowly, cautiously, she said, "Your wife was probably thrilled when she had twins, then."

Troy smiled. "Yeah. She was. Called them spices because she thought they were the spice of life."

"Ah," Sadie said, agreeing. If two kids could spice up anybody's life it would be Rosemary and Ginger.

"She would have been the perfect mother."

"And you miss her."

Troy blew his breath out on a sigh, leaned back in his chair and looked at the ceiling. "Like you would not believe."

"Try me," Sadie said, shifting forward on her chair to give him her full attention. This was the most relaxed she had ever seen him. With no demand on his time from Jake, no ringing phone, no twins disaster and contemplating his late wife, his face had softened. His guard was down. The weight of a bicoastal, multibillion-dollar business, a house full of staff and two precocious girls still sat on his shoulders, and Sadie suspected he never forgot that, but for at least a few minutes he was at ease. Very much like the sweet guy she remembered from high school.

"It's a complicated story," he said.

But his voice was heavy with longing, and Sadie immediately realized two things. First, he trusted her or he would have said no to her request, and second, though he protested, he didn't protest too hard and probably needed to talk about this.

"I would love to hear."

Troy tapped a pencil on the arm of his chair, seeming to consider what to say or perhaps if he should talk at all. Sadie prayed he would. She could see the pain in his eyes and in the tautness of his facial features. He needed to get some of this out. And she wanted to hear.

"There's not much to tell, but..."

He stopped because the den door inched open and Joni peeked inside. "Hi, I hope I'm not interrupting anything."

"No. No, come in," Troy said, quickly rising from his seat. He walked over to Joni, caught her elbow and guided her past the row of computers. "Is everything okay?"

"Yeah, everything's fine." She smiled at him, and though Sadie tried not to eavesdrop, it was hard not to notice the emotion shining from Joni's eyes when she was standing only a few feet away. "I'm just looking for some company."

"I'll be done with Sadie in a minute, then you and I can talk."

Joni smiled and nodded. Troy kissed her cheek. Sadie felt a fist of jealousy smash into her stomach. Getting a look at the real Troy these past few minutes helped her to understand her purely physical attraction wasn't a purely physical attraction. When he behaved like the guy she remembered, she liked him. That's what made the whole situation so confusing. Being nice seemed to come so naturally to him that it almost seemed he was hiding his real self from her. But why?

"Bruce should be in the kitchen. Get him to make you a snack and show you to the living room. I'll be right there."

The sick feeling of jealousy grew in Sadie's stomach, but she quickly squelched it. If there was one thing Troy Cramer needed it was a mother for his children. If there was a second thing he needed, it was a companion for himself. Sadie wasn't able to be either one. She might not care about the town's opinion of her anymore, but policewomen didn't marry billionaires. Maybe Troy realized that and behaved the way he did so she didn't get sucked into the fantasy. All along he might have understood what she was only now coming to realize. There was no point to them liking each other.

She rose. "You know what? Troy and I can talk about this tomorrow evening." Troy gave Sadie a quick look, but she glanced away and continued talking. "I need to get home. I have to work daylight tomorrow."

Joni's face brightened. "Oh, I thought you worked for Troy. You have another job, too?"

Before Sadie could answer Troy proudly said, "Sadie's a policewoman."

Joni gasped. "A policewoman!"

"Yes," Sadie said, for the first time doubting her sanity in choosing the career but just as quickly dropping that doubt. She loved her job. It was no longer of consequence that it shocked one of her high school friends to learn that she chose to investigate crimes, interrogate witnesses and protect the people of her hometown. Though it did reinforce that Sadie was not the right woman for Troy. She was an average, down-to-earth, rather simple woman, and any physical attraction she had to Troy was foolish. The Troy Cramers of the world needed the sleek, sophisticated, yet still kind and sweet Joni Somerses.

She smiled at Joni. "I suppose it is a surprise to see me in this kind of job. But I love my job, and I'm very good at it." She turned to Troy. "I'll be back tomorrow night."

"Actually, you'll be back tomorrow morning," Troy said. He faced Joni. "Go find Bruce while Sadie and I finish our discussion, and I'll catch up with you in the living room."

"Okay," Joni said. She smiled at Sadie. "We have to get together soon to talk." She winked. "Girl stuff."

"Right," Sadie said, returning Joni's smile, though she wasn't sure she could handle talking girl stuff with Joni if it included long conversations about her relationship with Troy. Still, she had never lost a friend over a man. Especially not one so clearly wrong for her. She didn't intend to start now. "Give me a call."

"I'm sure I'll see you around the estate," Joni said, gliding to the door, reminding Sadie that she was living here. In the house. With Troy. "We'll make plans then."

"Right," Sadie said, again reining in her jealousy.

"Let's sit," Troy said, taking Sadie's elbow to lead her to her chair after Joni left the room.

She shook off his hand. Her jealousy notwithstanding, the only reason she could think of that would cause Troy to ask Joni to leave the room was that he was about to tell Sadie something that would make her furious. "What did you do?"

"Well, you were so tired yesterday that I..."

Sadie gave him a scorching look.

"Well, I..."

Because he squirmed, she turned her scorching look up about fifty degrees.

Stuffing his hands in his trouser pockets, he sighed heavily. "All right, I called Chief Marshall. I told him I would buy him a new squad car if he would give you two weeks off."

"You what!"

"They get a squad car. The girls get the time they need with you. You get the time you need with them. It's win, win, win."

"It's insanity! How can you live like this?"

"I'm missing the problem here."

"First, you conveniently forgot about the fact that I was trying to keep working here a secret!"

His eyes widened with dismay. Then he squeezed them shut in agony. "Oh, God, Sadie, I'm sorry. The only excuse I have is that I do so much for so many different people sometimes things get jumbled or completely lost in the shuffle of my brain. I forgot."

"Don't worry about it. I faced down the crowd at the diner already this morning. My working here is no longer an issue."

Troy brightened. "It isn't?"

"No. Apparently somebody saw me get let into the gate last night. They drew the conclusion I was coming here for some kind of lovers' tryst. I told them I wasn't. They didn't believe me and they started to tease me. I told them to get a life and, *voilà*, it was over." She snapped her fingers. "Just like that."

"Just like that, huh?"

"It was simple, actually, and something I probably should have done years ago. But I think I had to be forced to see that there were worse fates in the world than getting teased. I think I had to want something badly enough that I would endure teasing for it. I had to be involved in something that really mattered."

"Being a policewoman doesn't matter?"

"It doesn't matter in the same way your girls matter, and that's the real bottom line here. By using your money to constantly get your own way, you're teach-

ing them that things, people, happiness can be bought.
And we both know that's not true. Rich people aren't
necessarily happy people.''

''No, but we show up for our problems in really
nice cars and looking really, really good.''

Sadie bit back a laugh. ''Very funny.''

Troy sighed. ''Look, Sadie, I'm sorry. I really am.
I was just trying to work it out so that everybody
would get what they need.''

''No, you were trying to work it out so that you
would get everything *you* want.''

''This isn't a question of what I want.''

''Actually, that's the most true thing you've said
since I started working for you. I'm not here to worry
about you or your life. I'm here for the girls,'' Sadie
said, remembering her talk with her mother and taking
advantage of the opportunity to turn the conversation
in the direction she wanted it to go. ''And your throwing around your money to make sure they get everything they want is a big part of their problem. Having
to wait for things, work for things or make do is what
makes life interesting. And sweet. And your daughters
are missing that. *You're* missing that.'' She turned and
headed for the office door, pleased with how the discussion had gone and realizing her mother was right.
Instead of him yelling at her, she got to paint the picture of his real life for him.

''I will see you tomorrow because I want to help
your girls. And because the town's opinion no longer
matters to me. I'm free. But you're not. You're trapped
by your money. Getting everything you want is not
always a good thing. And you know what? I feel sorry
for you. I feel even sorrier for your girls.''

* * *

Sadie was disappointed in him, and Troy's unhappiness resonated the whole way to his soul. Not because he needed her approval, but because she had made him realize he wasn't being as good a dad as he had thought he was. That shocked him so much that after Sadie's arrival the next morning he canceled his meetings for the day and changed into his swimming trunks. He didn't necessarily want to confront Sadie and make her explain her insinuations as much as he wanted time with his daughters when she was around so *he* could be the person to watch her and learn the things his daughters needed *him* to learn.

Troy pushed open the French doors leading to the patio. The three happy females playing in his pool didn't seem to notice him so he took his time, evaluating the scene.

Today Sadie wore a floral bathing suit of corals and pinks that heightened the darkness of her hair and the peachy tone of her skin. His girls also wore one-piece suits, but theirs were blue. For the first time, Troy noticed that the color made his daughters' eyes brighter. Or maybe it was having Sadie around that made their eyes brighter. They were playing, laughing, acting like little girls. Not sunbathing on a chaise longue like miniature divas, sipping soda, snapping their fingers for sunblock.

"Can I join you?"

"Dad!"

His squealed name echoed around him. As the girls bounced and splashed with delight, Troy signaled to Joe, who pulled his two-way radio from his belt and walked around a rhododendron bush. Since Troy typically didn't spend any daylight hours out of his office, he had given Joe the sign to alert Bruce that he was off schedule. At the same time, he let Joe know he could pull away from the girls, giving them privacy since their father was with them.

Troy tossed his towel to a chair and without hesitation dove into the water. When he surfaced, Rosemary and Ginger were already there.

"Don't you have work?" Ginger asked, then splashed his face.

"Yes and no," he said, skipping the heel of his hand across the water to return her splash. "Yes, I have work, but no, I don't want to do it."

"Race you to the other side!" Rosemary said, and immediately started swimming. Ginger dove in after her.

Troy gave his daughters a twenty-second head start, then smoothly cut through the water, making it to the other side long before they did. By the time they surfaced, he was leaning against the edge, examining his fingernails as if bored.

"Dad!"

"What? You said it was a race. I beat you fair and square."

"Your arms are bigger!"

"You never said anything about needing a handicap or a head start." He grimaced. "Frankly, I would be embarrassed to ask for one."

"Well, I wouldn't be," Sadie said, walking up behind Troy. She had put on her cover-up and sandals. "To win you always have to know your strengths, but you also should be aware of your weaknesses. If you need a handicap, take it. Never be afraid to ask for help."

That confused Troy so much, he turned to face her.

"Since when would *you* need a handicap or ask for help?"

"From the day I entered the police academy," Sadie replied, taking a seat on a chaise a few feet away. She began untangling the glistening strands of her hair with her fingers. "Being a cop takes brains, which I had, but I was definitely lacking in the brawn department. When I got to the police academy, I realized my shortcoming, found the best fighter in the group and made arrangements for him to tutor me."

"No kidding," Troy said, laughing.

Both his daughters gave him a confused look. "Why is that funny?" Rosemary asked.

"It isn't funny like ha-ha." Troy shifted uncomfortably in the water, feeling awkward that he'd given his daughter the wrong impression. "I'm laughing because I'm pleased. What Sadie did was very smart." He glanced at Sadie, expecting to get a smile of appreciation or approval, but instead the expectant look on her face condemned him. Clearly she wanted more from him.

"In a way I do the same thing," he said. He caught Sadie's gaze, hoping she would understand he wanted her to stay and show him what to do with his girls. "I hire experts. Then I take their advice."

"Is that what you're doing now?" Sadie countered, holding his gaze.

"Yes."

"Okay, then my advice is that there's more to life than work. There's play."

Troy nodded his understanding. He had a nearly nonexistent opportunity to play with his daughters, and she was telling him he should take it. Okay. That was what he had planned anyway, a little unscheduled time with his daughters. Then an idea popped in his head.

He turned toward his twins. "Get the big ball," he said, motioning to Ginger. "We'll play keep away."

"Three people isn't enough for a game of keep away!"

He faced Sadie. "Wanna play, Sadie?"

"No, I have to get going to work."

"But I—"

"You might have cleared my time off with the chief, but I promised Jimmy I would cover for him while he goes to the dentist. After today I'm all yours."

Though Troy didn't think she meant that in the way it came out, her comment sent a zing of excitement through him. He caught Sadie's gaze, but she quickly looked away. She was the most difficult female to understand. She was attracted to him, he was sure, but she wouldn't admit it. Of course, they couldn't really have a personal relationship. He wouldn't drag someone as independent as Sadie into his world of bodyguards and security. Still, he couldn't help but think how much fun having her in his world would be, because she was so lively, funny and interesting. But it was because he liked her so much that he knew he couldn't put her through it.

"I'll see you tomorrow then."

"Bye, Sadie!"

"Bye, Sadie!"

Though his bright-eyed daughters liked her, they didn't seem sorry to see her go because he was with them. A burst of love surged through him. He had forgotten how much they liked his company and how their love for him made him feel whole and strong and needed.

"Bye, Sadie," Troy echoed after his daughters, glad for the time alone with them and suddenly realizing what Sadie was doing. Giving them time alone wasn't merely good for the girls. It was good for *him,* too.

Obviously pleased that he'd taken the cue, Sadie smiled at him, said "Bye," and walked toward the French doors.

Troy turned his attention to his girls. "If you still want to play keep away, we can get Joe and Bruce to join us."

Rosemary's shoulders slumped. Ginger gave him a pained look. Troy quickly glanced at Sadie.

Her hand stopped midway to the doorknob, and she returned to the edge of the pool. "If you don't have enough people for keep away, and the girls want some private time with you, Troy," she said, not so subtly explaining the problem to Troy, "why don't you pick another game?"

"Like what?"

"Like fantasy island."

"Fantasy island?"

"Yeah, that's where you just tread water or back float and look up at the sky and try and figure out what the clouds are."

"The clouds are gas," Troy began, but Sadie cut him off with a look.

"I mean that you try to figure out what the clouds look like." She paused, pointed to a fluffy white cloud and said, "See that one there? To me it looks like a poodle."

Rosemary laughed. "It looks like two strawberries with whipped cream."

"No, it doesn't!" Ginger said, giggling. She threw herself to her back and floated, dreamily gazing skyward. "It looks like Bruce when he's kneading bread."

Rosemary and Sadie burst out laughing as Troy stared uncomprehendingly at the fluffy white cloud for a few seconds before he finally sighed. "I don't get it. A cloud is gas. That's all I see."

"And that," Sadie said, turning away, "is your problem. You only see the obvious. Which means you're missing a lot." She walked to the house, opened the French doors and slipped inside.

He looked at the sky. If he stopped seeing chemical symbols and numeric equations and only saw fluffy white wisps, he supposed he did see a poodle when he looked at the one cloud... "Clown. That one there," he said, pointing to the right. "It's a clown."

Rosemary giggled. "It's a beaver!"

"It's an Easter basket!" Ginger countered, laughing.

And suddenly Troy got the point of the game. It was to see the world through his daughters' eyes, to let them be kids, to let them dream. Bright eyed and smiling, they gazed at the sky like two happy little girls. And Troy knew Sadie was right. He was missing a lot.

"Joe!" he yelled as Rosemary floated on her back and Ginger treaded water, both of them gazing at the sky, both of them looking young and relaxed and incredibly like their mother.

Joe materialized from behind the rhododendron. "Yes?"

"Have Bruce call Sadie. I want her back here tonight at the house for dinner."

"But she's…"

"She's only working a few hours this afternoon," Troy said, interrupting him. "Just have Bruce find a time that's convenient for her." He nodded in the direction of his daughters. "I need to learn how to do more of this."

Joe looked at Troy's happy little girls and smiled. "I'll tell Bruce to make the arrangements."

The Silhouette Reader Service™ — Here's how it works:

If offer card is missing write to: Silhouette Reader Service, 3010 Walden Ave., P.O. Box 1867, Buffalo, NY 14240-1867

NO POSTAGE
NECESSARY
IF MAILED
IN THE
UNITED STATES

BUSINESS REPLY MAIL
FIRST-CLASS MAIL   PERMIT NO. 717-003   BUFFALO, NY

POSTAGE WILL BE PAID BY ADDRESSEE

SILHOUETTE READER SERVICE
3010 WALDEN AVE
PO BOX 1867
BUFFALO NY 14240-9952

Play the Romance Crossword Game

and get...
2 FREE BOOKS
and a
FREE GIFT...
YOURS to KEEP!

F R E E

Scratch Here!

to reveal the hidden words.
Look below to see what you get.

Yes!

I have scratched off the gold areas. Please send me my **2 FREE BOOKS** and **FREE GIFT** for which I qualify. I understand that I am under no obligation to purchase any books as explained on the back of this card.

315 SDL DRTQ   **215 SDL DRT6**

FIRST NAME   LAST NAME

ADDRESS

APT.#   CITY

STATE/PROV.   ZIP/POSTAL CODE

Visit us online at www.eHarlequin.com

ROMANCE	MYSTERY	NOVEL	GIFT
You get **2 FREE BOOKS** PLUS a **FREE GIFT!**	You get **2 FREE BOOKS!**	You get **1 FREE BOOK!**	You get a **FREE MYSTERY GIFT!**

Chapter Six

"If you don't like being summoned, I'm not sure I understand why you're going."

Sadie looked at her sister Hannah, who was sitting in the lotus position on Sadie's bed. With her blond hair and big green eyes, Hannah looked wholesome, fresh-faced and naive. But that suited her. As a small-town teacher who had never left home because she attended a local college, Hannah *was* naive.

"I'm going because I'm the girls' advocate. But, better yet, I'm going because I don't want to miss this chance."

Hannah's eyes narrowed with suspicion. "What chance?"

"To point out to Troy that by summoning me he's teaching the girls to be impatient and demanding."

"I thought you already did that?"

"I did, and it seemed to sink in. He was so good with his daughters today that it took me by surprise when he called me to his house like this."

Hannah tilted her head in question. Apparently having heard something in Sadie's tone, she said, "You like him."

Though Sadie knew it would have been better to give her sister an emphatic no to that comment, she couldn't seem to form the word. Especially not after seeing Troy in the pool with the twins. Like the night before when he was talking about his late wife, every ounce of arrogance had vanished. He was just a dad, trying to do the right thing with his daughters and working really hard because he was totally clueless. It was endearing. Sweet. She saw a side of Troy she knew existed when he was younger but thought he had lost as he became one of the smartest, wealthiest men in the country.

But whether or not she liked him was irrelevant because she finally understood that some of his early behavior had been a way of warning her off. Not only were policewomen and billionaires a bad mix, but he had a girlfriend.

She sighed and faced the mirror again. "How I feel about him doesn't matter. He has a girlfriend."

Hannah gasped. "He has a girlfriend?"

"Joni Somers is staying at his house. She's his HR director, but I get the impression she's more."

Reminded of Joni and realizing she would probably be at dinner, too, Sadie yanked her blue shirt over her head and stepped out of the blue skirt, then reached for her pink slip dress. She slid into the shear garment and faced the mirror.

Hannah sighed. "Wow. That looks great."

Sadie turned to the right, then the left, eyeing herself critically. "You think?"

"Sadie, pink is your color, and that dress is spectacular. I wish I had your…'' Hannah paused, struggling for the right word.

Sadie laughed. "You wish you had my figure."

"I wish I had just a little more in some places than what I have."

"It's a curse as much as a blessing. Look how hard I had to work to get people to take me seriously."

"They take you seriously now. Nobody at the diner will ever again cross you."

"They pushed me."

"Well, I hope that your little victory at the diner didn't make you overconfident. When you get to Troy's house make sure there wasn't a really good reason that he summoned you. Don't bite off his head without first finding out if he called you out there for a good reason."

Finally happy with her outfit, Sadie smiled at her sister. "He summoned me, Hannah, not more than twenty-four hours after I told him that kind of behavior is inappropriate for his daughters to see."

"But maybe his daughters didn't hear him order you—"

"It doesn't matter. The girls have already picked up on the behavior. Unless he stops acting like king of the world and shows them more appropriate ways to deal with people, they're going to spend their lives as two terrors with no friends and lead very miserable lives."

Having finished saying good-night to his daughters, Troy made his way upstairs from the basement family room and into the kitchen. "They're ready for you."

Bruce hefted a tub of popcorn. "And I'm ready for them."

"Are you sure this is a good idea?"

"Ninety percent of the kids in the United States would kill for a night of horror movies on their own movie screen. In some circles your girls are considered very lucky. This is a primo example."

"You're sure?"

"I'm positive."

"And we're not damaging their little psyches?"

"If we are, it will be the last time."

"Yeah." Troy grimaced. "I'm just about certain that once I tell Sadie I want to hear everything she has to say about what I'm doing wrong with my daughters, she's going to open the floodgates. If horror movies are bad, we'll know."

Bruce chuckled. "I think you can count on it."

"Okay. So, you'll watch the movies with them..."

"Until they fall asleep, then I'll carry them to bed. Your evening is your own."

"Unless I finish early."

"I sincerely doubt it. Once Officer Evans realizes she's got your complete attention, I'm sure she'll have plenty to say."

Troy winced. "Right. I'll see you tomorrow then."

After checking on the dinner Bruce had prepared—a peace offering, Bruce had suggested, to keep Sadie at least reasonably pleasant through the chat—he walked outside to the patio to make sure everything was set up there. The round glass table had been covered with an airy cloth, decorated with a vase of flowers and set with good china and silver. Frosted globes provided just enough light to see and not so much that they spoiled the serenity of the carefully designed patio. He hit a switch, and soft music floated onto the warm night air.

He wasn't specifically trying to soothe a savage beast. But he remembered Sadie's sarcastic streak and her temper. Plus, he had worked to make sure she stayed angry with him as a way for him to control his attraction to her, giving her every reason in the world to be testy with him. He had hired her to get help with the girls, yet almost every time she tried to give him advice, he argued with her or something happened to prevent her from having her say.

If she was angry with him or cautious about giving her suggestions and directions, he deserved it, which meant he needed to show her he was not only apologetic, he was also receptive to hearing everything she had to say. He was sure the dinner, soft lights and mellow music spelled receptive, open, warm. I'm your guy. I'm ready to listen. Help me.

As far as Troy was concerned, everything was perfect.

Right on time his front doorbell rang. With Bruce in the basement with the girls, Joe off for the evening and Jake entertaining Joni by showing her how the area had changed since she lived here, Troy was on his own. He turned and ran to the front door.

When he opened it, his mouth fell open. "Sadie?"

The soft pink dress she wore didn't merely accent the rich hue of her dark hair, it also showcased a figure most men would consider absolutely perfect.

"You dressed up."

She gaped at him. "You didn't."

He glanced at his trousers and casual shirt. "No."

"But you invited me for dinner!"

A million thoughts jumped to his mind, forty conclusions begged for attention, but one muscled its way to the forefront. In spite of the way he had treated her, she liked him. At least a little.

He grinned. "You dressed up to have dinner with me?"

"No, I dressed up to have dinner at your house. With Joni... Remember? You have a houseguest. I didn't want to look like a slouch."

Because no one would ever accuse Sadie of looking like a slouch, Troy thought about that for a second— but only a second—before he realized she wasn't concerned about dinner being a dress-up event as much as she was worried about how she would compare to Joni. "You're jealous?"

"Ha!" she said, walking into the foyer when he stepped back to invite her inside. "Fat chance."

Troy closed the door, turned and grinned at her again. "Whatever," he singsonged, reminding himself of the twins.

"Don't 'whatever' me. I dressed because I didn't know how the infamous Troy Cramer and company had dinner. If you don't like the dress, I can take it off."

"By all means."

"Down, Fido. I have a spare uniform in the car. I'm not going to eat naked."

"My loss," he said, then laughed heartily. He'd never seen her upset or even slightly unnerved, but he had her off balance, and it thrilled him. Since she'd come to work for him she always had the upper hand. She had barged into his household like a bulldog who grabbed everybody by the ankle and had no intention of letting go. Even Bruce was a tad afraid of her. Now, suddenly, she was off balance, and he was the one standing on solid ground.

"We're eating on the patio."

Head high, she began to march in that direction. "Good."

Troy had to race to keep up with her, ready for another small battle when she saw the dim lights and soft music. God only knew how she would take them, but he was just about certain she wouldn't be pleased.

He reached the French doors and stopped on the threshold. Sadie stood on his patio, the glow of the frosted lights illuminating her satiny skin and soft music drifting around her. She looked confused, dumbfounded and absolutely beautiful.

When she realized he was standing in the doorway she faced him. "Are you trying to seduce me?"

"Never." He stuffed his hands in his trouser pockets, intending to look cool and unaffected and keep the conversation light. But the truth was since she had all but admitted she cared for him by being jealous and dressing to kill, he suddenly wished he *could* seduce her.

"Where's Joni?"

"Out with Jake."

She shot him a puzzled look. "Out with Jake?"

He stepped away from the French doors and onto the brick patio. "They seemed to really hit it off."

"And you let them?"

"Of course, I let them. They're two of my closest friends. I would love to see them hook up."

"You're not jealous?"

"From where I'm standing you're handling everything in the jealousy department nicely."

"Right."

"Come on, admit it. You thought she was my girlfriend and it drove you crazy."

"The only thing that drives me crazy is the fact that your daughters' lives are a mess."

"And that's why you're here for dinner. I want to fix that."

"You've said that before, yet look what you did tonight. You summoned me to dinner."

He grimaced. "Oh, geez. I didn't even realize I had done that."

"That's because you're accustomed to having everyone jump when you say jump. You're the boss. You expect people to drop everything and do what you want. And that's why it's hard for me to believe you'll listen to a word I say."

"I swear, I will. I have a whole different perspective than when I hired you. I'm ready to hear everything you have to say."

She turned. "Really?"

He held his hands out in defeat. "Really."

"And that's what this is all about?" she said, motioning around the patio to the dim lights, soft music and cloth-covered table.

"Completely." He took a few steps toward her. "Dinner is a peace offering." He paused and caught her gaze. "Bruce's idea. He figured if we broke bread we could be civil, since he knows we sometimes don't get along."

"Okay," she said, not sounding too convinced that the dinner was innocent.

Troy almost began to explain again. Almost. But he didn't. One slipped word, one longing glance, and the entire dynamic of this evening could change. Already his feelings for her were shifting, deepening, all because the way she dressed proved she had feelings for him. They were standing on very dangerous ground, and Troy had to make sure they kept their footing. If they didn't, he could fall in love with her. Then he would be in the same boat he was in when Angelina died, because Sadie wouldn't stay in this life forever. It was hard to be surrounded by bodyguards, hard not to be able to do a lot of the things normal people did. Sadie might like him, but when she discovered how difficult his life was, she would leave.

And he wouldn't blame her.

He pulled a bottle of wine from the bucket by the table. "Drink?"

She turned from staring at the pool. "Huh?"

"Would you like a glass of wine?"

"I'm driving."

"One glass before dinner won't hurt."

Her eyes narrowed, as if she was considering that he might be trying to get her drunk and take advantage of her.

Troy replaced the bottle. "You know what? Maybe you're right. No wine for you."

Her eyes narrowed again. Troy almost shook his head at her very suspicious nature, but he didn't. Instead, he found himself drowning in the gaze of her perfect green eyes, being tempted to do the things she seemed to be expecting him to do. But he wouldn't. He knew he couldn't.

He headed for the French doors. "I'll just go in and get the salads."

She gaped at him. "No servant?"

"I told you. This is an informal dinner. A chance for you and me to talk about the girls. Nothing more."

"Right." She smiled at him, then glanced around as if confused that she could have read everything so wrong.

"I'll only be a minute."

Troy headed for the kitchen. Once the swinging door closed behind him, he leaned against the butcher block, praying for strength. The scene was set. She expected him to seduce her. He suspected she wouldn't put up too much of a fight.

But he couldn't do it. He couldn't risk getting involved with her—and likely losing her. On the other hand, he wouldn't risk hurting her by pulling her into his difficult life, forcing her to give up her hard-won independence, forcing her to choose between him and her freedom.

He grabbed the salads, composed himself, then stepped onto the patio again.

"It's just a simple garden salad. Nothing fancy. We didn't even use Romaine lettuce."

"That's fine."

"Good," he said. His arm accidentally brushed her arm when he served her salad. Tingles shot through his muscles, but he ignored them, keeping his face blank, his demeanor casual. He couldn't have her. Not permanently. Sooner or later she would rebel like Angelina did and then she would be gone. He didn't think she would die as his wife had, but he did know she would run. For her own sanity, she would leave him. Then he would not only face the loneliness of love lost, but she would feel guilty about leading him on and abandoning the girls. His keeping the relationship platonic was more for her benefit than his. And that realization made it easy for him to behave.

He offered her dressing. "French, ranch or blue cheese?"

"Blue cheese," she said, taking the appropriate ladle. "So, you're ready to hear about what you're doing wrong with the girls?"

"Absolutely. Start at the beginning and give it to me straight."

"First, they have access to too much money."

"Easily fixed."

"They also shouldn't be able to order around Bruce and Joe. Bruce and Joe should be guiding them."

"Bruce and Joe might have trouble with that."

"They shouldn't. They're adults. Adults are supposed to guide children. It doesn't work the other way around. Yet your kids think it should."

"Okay. I see what you're saying, but I have no clue how to fix it. Do you have any ideas?"

"Only about thirty," Sadie said and began to outline ways Bruce and Joe could take the lead with the girls rather than the other way around.

Troy sat forward, giving her his complete attention, listening to every way he had inadvertently screwed up with his kids and every idea she had for how to fix things. He refused to notice how green her eyes were or how lovingly she spoke of his daughters.

Wrapped in the warmth of her tone, he realized something his attraction to her had been overshadowing. She cared about his daughters. Really cared. He stifled the surge of longing that rose up in him. Then wondered if he wasn't making a mistake by keeping his distance tonight. Not because he had changed his mind and believed he could have a permanent, long-term relationship with Sadie. He knew he couldn't. Not because he thought he could have a fling with her. He wouldn't risk her heart that way. Besides, tonight he didn't need that much from her.

He was lonely for company, conversation, someone who cared.

The night was warm and inviting, and they were friends. Surely, they could enjoy each other's company for one night. Surely it wasn't out of line to laugh and talk, maybe even dance. Just once.

They talked about strategies for shifting the relationship between Joe and Bruce and the twins the whole way through the salad. By the time Troy served the entrée—spaghetti—Sadie felt a little less self-conscious about being dressed up when he wasn't. She had also gotten over the fact that he guessed she was jealous. Not because there was no more reason to be jealous, since Joni was out with Jake, but because her jealousy was wrong and pointless. She had no intention of getting involved with Troy.

He returned with the spaghetti, and through the meal they chatted about giving the girls an allowance and the benefits of assigning them chores, even if it was only cleaning their bedroom. When Troy offered her dessert, she refused.

"I'm stuffed. Bruce is a wonderful cook."

"Italian food is his specialty." Troy rose and gathered their dishes. "Are you sure you don't want dessert or coffee?"

She smiled. "I'm sure."

He left to take the plates into the kitchen, and Sadie sat back sated and happy, more comfortable with him than she'd been since they originally made this arrangement. Though he frequently behaved like an overbearing, overly spoiled corporate executive, he could also be a normal guy. And she wasn't lying to herself anymore. She really liked the normal guy. He wasn't just easy to talk to. He also wanted to be a really good dad.

Troy returned empty-handed. As he stepped through the French doors onto the patio, he said, "So tell me about your last boyfriend."

"Zippy?"

As Troy took his seat, he frowned. "Zippy… Your boyfriend from high school was your last boyfriend?"

Sadie laughed. "No, I was teasing, seeing if you would remember. My last boyfriend was the guy from the police academy who taught me how to fight. We had a long, passionate affair the whole way through our training, then I moved to Pittsburgh and he moved to Idaho and it didn't work out long distance."

"That makes sense."

"It still hurt to lose him," Sadie said—with a laugh, because as nice as Troy was, he frequently looked at life a little too logically.

"I'm sure it did, but I'm also sure you didn't just drop dead because of one failed relationship."

"No, I dated in Pittsburgh," Sadie said casually, because she felt very comfortable telling him. All through dinner he had proved he wasn't trying to put the moves on her. He really was a nice guy interested in helping his daughters. And it felt good to talk to someone who had known her way back when she was immature and appreciated that she was different without making her feel she should apologize for having been a teenager.

"But dating in the city is odd. No relationship seems to last more than six weeks. The usual ritual is that I find somebody who has the same interest I do, like waterskiing, and when the season is over so is the relationship. Right before I moved home, I finally decided I needed to find a hobby I could do all year so I could see if that didn't make a relationship last.''

Troy laughed.

"I'm serious."

"I see that. I'm laughing because it seems a lot of plotting goes into relationships these days.''

Sadie sighed. "Yeah." She paused, then slowly raised her eyes to meet his gaze. "But it's necessary. It's not like you can date somebody who is already your friend.''

Troy shook his head. "No, you can't. Because then you risk losing your friend.''

"I've done that."

"I never have, but that's because I haven't been in the dating arena long. Before I was married, the only woman I seriously dated was my wife. Now that I'm single again, I have a different agenda. My life is so complicated with bodyguards and security that I don't want to get another woman involved. So my relationships, when I have them, are very casual. Which means not dating my friends is doubly important.''

She nodded. He couldn't have been any clearer if he had written this out in a note. He liked her as a friend. She was safe with him. That disappointed her, making her realize she wanted a relationship with him, but she understood what he was saying about his life. It wouldn't be easy to take Bruce or someone like him everywhere she went. Still, that didn't mean they couldn't be friends.

"I think I would like a cup of coffee."

When Troy returned with a tray containing a silver coffeepot and delicate china cups, a soft, romantic instrumental was drifting through the night air. He set the tray on the table and put his hand on the back of her chair. "This is such a nice song, it seems a shame to waste it."

Understanding that he intended for them only to be friends, Sadie wasn't sure if she should argue. Before she got the chance he took her hand and tugged gently, urging her from her chair. Then, before panic hit her that their dancing might be outside the boundaries of what friends do, he began talking about his daughters again.

"So, we agree on the allowance. We agree about giving them chores. But I'm still a little skeptical about sending them to Wilburn Elementary."

She drew back as if surprised. "They would love it."

"I'm sure they would. They'd terrorize the teachers and wrap all the kids around their little fingers by bribing them."

"Well, they did learn from the master."

"Very funny."

Sadie laughed. "Sorry, I couldn't resist."

And Troy felt as if he couldn't resist, either. Though he knew they could only be friends, the night was warm, enticing. And Sadie felt wonderful in his arms. Without realizing he was doing it, he pulled her closer. Amazingly, she didn't contest. He nestled his jaw against her temple.

"The truth is, Troy, the residents of Wilburn aren't as easily manipulated as you might think they are."

"I'm not so much worried about them as I am my daughters. In a school like Briarhills, everybody's even. In a school like Wilburn Elementary, wealth will make my kids an exception. I'm afraid Ginger and Rosemary might actually be enticed into trying to use money to get their own way."

Sadie shook her head. "I don't think there will be a problem. The local kids might not be rich, but they're just as competitive as the students at Briarhills. Your girls won't buy a spot on a volleyball team that wants to make it into the finals, and they also won't buy first place in the spelling bee. Frankly, Troy, in a world where most people don't have money it's entirely possible your money will be meaningless."

Troy didn't know if that was true, and he wished he had the brainpower to think about it. But he didn't. He was focused on how nicely she fit against him, how logical she sounded, how wonderful it was to have someone to really talk to without worry about her motives or intentions. Amazingly, it was the last realization that made him recognize what she said *was* true. "That's why my money means nothing to you."

She pulled far enough away that she could catch his gaze. "It's not that I don't have any. But I certainly can't compete with yours. So I try to make you play the game according to my rules."

"Well, you devil."

She smiled softly, and Troy felt the smile the whole way to his toes. For the first time in two years, he felt completely attuned to another person, a woman, a mate. And he could see from the look in her eyes, the soft smile on her lips that she felt the same way.

Though he had promised himself he wouldn't kiss her, he lowered his head and gently touched his mouth to her lips. This time, instead of feeling a thunder of sexual attraction, he felt the warmth of emotion. Sadie was someone who knew him, someone who cared about him, someone about whom he cared more than he realized until this second. And every ounce of emotion they had for each other was there in the press of their mouths. They weren't giving in to passion, though it was there, hovering beneath the surface and eager to spring to life. They were expressing something deeper, something more wonderful.

He let go of her fingers and drew Sadie into a full-fledged embrace. Her hands smoothed up his shirt to catch behind his neck. His hands reverently glided along the curve of her waist, teased by the soft texture of her dress, knowing her skin was a hundred times more delectable. He pulled her closer, luxuriating in finally getting to touch her.

And she wasn't resisting.

The thought snapped his control, and a frisson of arousal burst through him. He yanked her nearer, gratified when she deepened the kiss. Her lips parted, allowing him access to the sweet recesses of her mouth, and Troy felt himself spiraling away from reality. But the sound of something crashing to the stone floor brought him back to reality with a jolt.

Troy and Sadie broke apart like guilty teenagers, but one even more guilty person stood in suspended animation beside the broken vase. Her guilty twin stooped wide-eyed beneath the table, peeking around the tablecloth as if it were a veil.

"What are you doing?"

Both twins stayed frozen.

"And how long have you been there?"

"We—" Ginger began.

But Troy interrupted her. "You're supposed to be in the screening room with Bruce!"

Rosemary perked up. "We fell asleep," she said, obviously believing that excuse saved her and Ginger from punishment.

"At..." Troy glanced at his watch, but it was almost ten. Funny how the time had passed. "Never mind the time. The point is, you should be in bed."

"We were!" Rosemary said.

"We were!" Ginger seconded. "But I woke up—"

"And dragged your sister down here?"

Sadie touched her fingers to Troy's forearm. "Uh, Troy. The situation with the movie and them waking up has been explained. The big issue now is how they got under the table without us noticing."

Troy's eyes narrowed menacingly. "How did you get under the table? How did you get out to the patio without either of us noticing?"

Ginger crawled out from under the table. "You know the secret place that Bruce made for us to hide in case something bad happens?"

Troy groaned. "You used those stairs!"

Both twins nodded.

"You're not allowed to use those stairs! No one's supposed to know about those stairs!" Troy rubbed his hand across his mouth. "That's it. Back to your rooms! We will definitely talk about this in the morning."

"You should talk about it now," Sadie said, indicating with her eyes that this was one of the things he couldn't put off. She gathered her purse from the table and began walking toward the patio door.

He caught her hand to stop her, then faced his daughters. "Go upstairs and wait for me. We need to finish our discussion." They nodded and raced into the house. Troy turned to Sadie. "Don't go."

"I have to."

"You won't stay and coach me through this?"

Sadie laughed. "Now that you know the problem, you'll do fine."

"But I like having you help me."

"I'm not sure my being with you is a good idea."

Troy knew she was right. If he wanted her to continue helping him with his daughters, she couldn't play mom and they shouldn't kiss. They definitely shouldn't dance again.

He let go of her hand, and she left him standing alone on his patio. Soft music still drifted around him. The scent of his gardens filled the air. And the knowledge that she was right bothered him. They still had a week, maybe two, of her working in his house, helping his daughters. If they got too close, Troy had a feeling he was going to be the one who ended up with the broken heart.

Chapter Seven

After his chat with the twins, Troy headed for the living room, but changed his mind and went to his office. He knew it would be quiet there, and it seemed important to be among the things he understood—reports, memos, financial statements and computers.

He didn't turn on the overhead light but opted for the brass lamp on his desk. It gave enough of a glow to the room that he wasn't precisely sitting in the dark but provided so little light that he felt as if he were in his own private world.

Which was ironic, he thought, as he fell into the burgundy leather chair, given that living in his own private little world was the problem. He had worked most of his life to achieve this level of success, not for the money but to do his part to bring the world to the next level of progress. A person couldn't be gifted with intelligence and ability and ignore his calling. Yet his life would have been so much simpler if he had.

If he were a normal person with a normal life, he would be pursuing Sadie right now.

"So here you are!"

Troy looked up to see Joni standing in the doorway. Dressed in jeans and a cute T-shirt, with her gorgeous blond hair streaming around her, he knew she was every man's fantasy come to life. But even if she sat on his lap and kissed him, he wouldn't have reacted. To him, Sadie had become the epitome of beauty and femininity.

"What's the matter? Why are you back here all by yourself, sitting in the dark?" Joni asked, lighting the floor lamp and the lamp on the coffee table in front of the leather sofa as she entered the room.

"I'm just tired."

"I think it's more than that."

Amused by her perceptiveness, he looked up and smiled. "Really?"

"Yes. I know you think that being overwhelmed by my own troubles would prevent me from seeing yours, but I'm not blind."

"I don't have any troubles."

"Sure you do. In fact, that's actually why you brought me here."

He raised an eyebrow. "Really."

She smiled knowingly. "I have it all figured out." She paused, considered what she had said and amended it. "Well, I have most of it figured out. I think you brought me here to make sure there was no romance between you and Sadie. I'm just not sure if my presence was supposed to make you behave or to scare Sadie off."

He laughed. "Actually, you're right. Initially, I did bring you here to keep things platonic between Sadie and me. Since I'm usually very proper around my staff, I had hoped having you around would remind me I was supposed to behave."

"Didn't work?"

He shook his head. "Nope. Not that it makes a difference. I told her tonight that I would never date a friend because I wouldn't want to risk losing one. She understood what I said, and I'm sure things will remain platonic between us."

Joni frowned. "Really?"

"Yes."

"I'm surprised that you're giving up so easily."

"No, I'm surprised that I let things go so far when I knew it was wrong."

Joni laughed. "You let things go, Troy, because you're falling in love."

"Right. I've known her all of a week."

"Oh, Troy, you've known Sadie all your life. You loved her through high school. She has grown up, but the important parts of her personality haven't changed. She's still a good, decent woman who also happens to be gorgeous. I would bet the moment you saw her for the first time after being apart so long, your heart skipped a beat."

He smiled. "More than my heart skipped a beat."

"Then you have to fight for this."

"Wrong. I need to walk away while I can."

Joni gaped at him. "But Sadie is perfect for you!"

He shook his head. "That might be true, but this situation is a lot more complicated than you think."

Joni gave him a knowing look. "Really? You think I don't get it? Your young, beautiful wife was taken from you so suddenly it threw you into shock. I watched you go through three months of agony before you could pull yourself together enough that you could work. And you think I don't understand that you don't want to go through that again?"

He tossed the pencil he had been twirling to the desk. "No. I don't."

"But, Troy, there's no law that says you're going to."

Troy stared at her. "Do you really think Sadie could live this life? Give up her job? Give up her freedom? My God, Joni, you've seen how independent she is."

"Yes, but you can't make this choice for her by simply walking away."

"I also can't blindly walk into a bad situation. Lots of people depend on me. The company is bigger than it was when Angelina died. If I end up hurt again I'm not sure Sunbright would survive the inattention it would suffer while I wallowed in misery."

"So don't get hurt."

Troy shook his head in confusion. "You're not really being helpful. There's no way I can prevent myself from being hurt. If I do what I think you're suggesting, and Sadie and I date, while Sadie is trying to figure out if she can handle the way I live, I'll be falling in love. I'll be setting myself up for the heartache of a lifetime when she realizes she can't do it and leaves without so much as a backward glance."

Joni rose. "Sadie won't do that to you."

"No. She won't, because I'm not going to give her the chance. We haven't really started anything yet. As long as I stay away from her, we will both be fine."

The next morning, Bruce stepped into Troy's office. "I'm sorry to interrupt you, boss, but Joni asked for a breakfast tray, and when I delivered it she told me to tell you that she won't be working today. She's sick.''

Troy looked up. "How sick?"

Bruce shrugged. "She seemed to be okay, but she was sniffling. I'm guessing she has a cold.''

"Okay, Bruce, thanks.''

Bruce nodded and left, and Troy went back to work. Then he remembered that tonight was the night of the senator's party in Atlanta. A party he had to attend. A party Joni had promised to attend as his date. Then he panicked.

He could not go without a date. The thought of eager mothers trying to fix him up with their daughters, sad looks from people who knew his life story and lectures he would get about not stopping to smell the roses filled him with dread. It would be the most miserable four hours of his life, and the ramifications would be exponential. If people thought he had trouble getting dates, acquaintances would play matchmaker for years. Friends would offer invitations for ski trips and gambling excursions to get him out of his house and back to the land of the living. He wouldn't get a minute's peace.

"Hey, Troy," Jake said, entering the office. "What's the odd look for?"

Troy sat back in his chair. "Would you believe I have a party at Senator Sanders's house tonight and no date?"

"I thought you were taking Joni."

"She's sick."

He frowned. "Too bad," he said as he sat on one of the chairs in front of Troy's desk. "Guess you'll have to go alone."

"It's awkward when I go alone. People feel they

need to fix me up, lecture me about working too much or they decide that I am for some reason to be pitied."

Jake grinned. "I have a little black book."

"Sweet. I would love to take a stripper from Biloxi to meet the head of the joint chiefs of staff."

"Hey, none of them are strippers. My ex-girlfriends even include some fairly high-profile celebrities."

"I'm sorry. I didn't mean that like it sounded."

"I know you didn't. But if you won't take my little black book, I have another suggestion."

Troy sighed with relief. "Great."

"Since Joni's sick, take Sadie."

Troy laughed mirthlessly. "Not on your life."

"Why not?"

"Because he likes her," Joni said, entering the room dressed in a long terry-cloth robe and blowing her nose. "And he's afraid if he spends time with her he'll like her more than he already does."

"I don't think you have to worry about that," Jake said, turning from Joni to Troy. "I got the impression from Luke this morning that you did a really good job of warning Sadie off last night. I think if you explained that you needed a date, that everything you said last night still stood and that you were desperate, she would help you."

"I think Jake's right," Joni said, then blew her nose. "But I think it would work even better if you let me talk to her."

"I can't handle this myself?" Troy asked, skeptically.

"Well, you could, but I think it would come across as being more of a favor if I set it up for you. You know, if I asked her to go with you to replace me as a favor to *me,* not as a favor to *you.*"

Unfortunately, that made sense to Troy. And he did believe what Jake reported from Sadie's brother. Troy had warned Sadie off enough the night before that neither of them would do anything foolish. There would be no repeat of the kiss or the dancing.

He caught Joni's gaze. "Okay. Do it. But be nice. Don't make her feel she has to go with me. She's kind of been on my case lately about pushing people around, and I'm trying to mend my ways."

Jake laughed, but Joni nodded and scampered out of the room.

Standing by the white brick fireplace in the living room of a home that looked very much like it could have been pulled from the pages of *Gone With The Wind,* Sadie kept a firm grip on her wineglass to prevent her hand from shaking. The dress Joni had lent her was a backless, strapless, black silk gown. Fitted at the bodice, it rode roughshod along her curves because she was more full-figured than Joni. Then it fell in a tight straight line to the floor. Joni had also provided black gloves, and a diamond bracelet that probably cost more than Sadie made in two years.

Because the dress fit so well and was perfect for her coloring, Sadie felt decadently beautiful. Standing beside Troy, who looked intense and masterful in his black tuxedo, she didn't feel one whit out of place.

And that was what scared her.

"Senator," Troy said as a tall, thin man in his fifties approached them. "I would like to introduce my friend, Sadie Evans."

The man took her hand and kissed her fingers. "It's a pleasure."

"The pleasure is mine," she said, smiling first at

him, then at Troy. But glancing at Troy was a big mistake. He was staring at her with so much affection and approval shining from the depths of his enticing blue eyes that she couldn't seem to look away.

"I'm guessing the two of you are more than friends," the senator said with a laugh.

Troy held Sadie's gaze for another second, then he looked at the senator and said, "We're just friends. Former biology lab partners."

"No kidding!" Charlie Sanders said, chuckling again.

"I was a bit of a conniver in high school," Sadie confessed, getting Troy's message loud and clear because he had been sending it all night. *Don't like me. Don't want me. Keep this simple.* "I didn't exactly study, and Troy was the smartest kid in town."

"Now Troy appears to be one of the smartest kids in the universe," the senator said, expertly shifting the conversation from pleasure to business. "My committee has been wondering if you've taken a look at that schematic we sent you."

Sadie wasn't surprised that the comment was just vague enough to keep her out of the loop and specific enough for Troy to answer. That was the way the conversations had been all evening. Having the discussions go over her head didn't insult her as much as it alerted her to the fact that Troy's life was very different than what everybody thought. He didn't plan, create and think only for himself. Everybody wanted a piece of his brain.

The conversation with the senator proved Troy was important. He didn't merely use his knowledge to make money. He sincerely wanted to do what he could to benefit society.

A strong protective instinct rose in her. Troy might not want to hurt her, and she might not want to get hurt, but no one, it seemed, protected him. No one cared about him. Everybody cared about his brain. But not *him*.

She shifted closer and slid her fingers under his hand where it rested by his thigh. Obviously preoccupied with the conversation, Troy absently entwined his fingers with hers.

And Sadie got the final click. The final piece of understanding. He didn't merely need someone to accompany him, someone to make love with him or even help him raise his kids. He needed someone who understood him, someone who loved him, someone who could share his difficult life. And she could. Tears filled her eyes. Worse, she really really wanted to. Because she loved him, she hated the fact that he went through the stress of being pursued for help and running his own company alone.

The evening progressed in the same manner in which it had begun. Sadie didn't feel she was attending a dinner party as much as a consultation. By the time they were able to leave the white-pillared mansion and head for their limousine, Troy was clearly exhausted.

He handed her into the back seat and took his place beside her, then a uniformed chauffeur closed the door.

Sadie shifted closer, wrapped her hands around his arm and laid her head on his shoulder. "I'm sorry."

"What?"

"I really, really, really had your life all wrong."

Troy chuckled. "You got all that from a four-hour dinner?"

"No, I got all that from the questions the senator asked but didn't ask. The request the sultan made without saying anything. And the butt-kissing the banker did without throwing himself at your feet."

Troy laughed again. "You weren't supposed to be analyzing these people, you were supposed to be charming them."

"Huh! Like you need help getting people to like you."

"Sadie, these guys don't like me. If they weren't pursuing me, they would be looking for the guy behind me at MIT, or the kid graduating this year who knows a hundred times more than I do because he's been playing on a computer since he was six months old."

"They don't come to you for just your brain, Troy. They come to you for your experience. You have an experienced brain."

That made him laugh.

But Sadie didn't think any of this was funny, and deep down, she knew Troy didn't, either. She swallowed hard and made a decision that she wasn't sure was the right one. She only knew it was the one her heart was urging her to make.

"Everybody wants you for your brain except me," she whispered, hoping he'd heard, not sure she was able to say the words any louder.

He shifted on the seat so he could look at her. "Sadie, don't…"

"I like you," she said quickly, interrupting him before he could give her the lecture from the night before. "I'm not asking for a commitment. I'm not even asking for anything permanent. I just like you enough that I would like to be part of your life for a while."

Her answer seemed to relieve him. "You are part

of my life. And, more important, you're part of my girls' lives.''

''I want to be more than that.''

''You can't.''

''Why not?''

''Because it doesn't work for me.''

Sadie held his gaze. Staring into his blue eyes, she saw the sadness, the need he could so easily deny with words, and realized he was deliberately misinterpreting her. She leaned forward and gently touched her mouth to his, believing that he might be able to verbally deny his feelings but he wouldn't be able to resist a kiss. But he didn't respond.

Anger shivered through her. Not because he was rejecting her, but because he was denying himself, and she knew he was doing it to protect her. She shifted closer and pressed her lips harder against his. When he still didn't respond, she steadied herself with her hands on his shoulders and moved until her breasts pressed against his chest as her mouth moved softly against his. Again, nothing.

In the last second, the second when she was about to give up hope, he clasped her shoulders and hauled her against him, kissing her deeply. As if something inside him snapped, his tongue tumbled into her mouth, his lips devoured her, his hands raced along her naked back.

Sadie thought she would die from the sheer pleasure of it. Sensation after sensation trembled through her. Not from the pure physical delights, but because she loved him.

She loved him.

She understood him and she loved him and she wanted to make love to him.

"Mr. Cramer?"

The voice from the intercom interrupted them. Troy stopped. Sadie froze.

"We're at the airport, sir."

Troy shifted Sadie away from him. Sadie drew a quick breath. "How can we be at the airport already? It took us twenty minutes to get to the senator's house when we arrived. The return trip can't take ten!"

"Nigel moved the plane."

"What?"

"He moved the plane," Troy said, pulling a handkerchief from his suit pocket. Coolly, impersonally, he began to remove the lipstick from his mouth.

Remorse and regret overwhelmed her. He couldn't help but return her kiss, but he wished he hadn't. And for the first time Sadie noticed something about Troy that she had seen before but hadn't acknowledged. He was very, very strong. If he made up his mind that they wouldn't have a relationship, then they wouldn't.

"Moving my plane is a safety precaution."

Sadie glanced away as she nodded her understanding. Tears pricked her eyes. Damn it! He had warned her to stay away from him, to keep things impersonal, but she just couldn't listen. She reached for the door handle, but Troy caught her hand.

"Sadie, don't."

"I'm just getting out of the car."

"No, I mean don't be upset. I wanted to kiss you. You wanted to kiss me."

Even more embarrassed because he felt he had to explain to make her feel better, Sadie said, "Right."

"But this thing between us," he began, but he stopped and drew a long breath. "No, let me start over. I meant what I said last night. I don't want a permanent relationship. I was very hurt when my wife died.''

"I understand.''

He shook his head. "No, you don't. Look around you, Sadie. You are in a bulletproof car. You will be surrounded by plainclothes bodyguards as we walk to my private plane. Which had to be moved from one airport to another to preclude sabotage. Things are set up this way because there is an element of danger to being me.''

"I'm a policewoman, Troy. I know exactly how much danger there is to your life.''

"And I won't expose you to it.''

She drew a long breath. "And maybe as a smart woman I shouldn't want to be exposed.''

Sadie said the words she knew would make Troy happy and was rewarded by another of his relieved smiles. But inside her heart was breaking. Not for herself, but for him.

He would live alone, bear his burdens alone, because he wouldn't risk that another woman he married would be hurt.

She understood.

She agreed.

She hated it.

She hated the knowledge that she would never make love to him, never share his life. It hurt so much that tears stung her eyes for the entire flight home, and she was glad Troy pretended to be sleeping.

Chapter Eight

When Sadie arrived at Troy's house the next morning, Bruce was waiting for her in the foyer. "Mr. Cramer wants to see you in the living room."

"Okay," Sadie said, realizing he had summoned her as an employee because he was further drawing the line, making sure she understood there would be nothing between them. It hurt, but she knew making an issue of it would only embarrass her. He was strong. Determined. Sadie wouldn't change his mind.

Forcing herself to smile, she walked into the living room. When she saw the woman seated on the over-stuffed chair across from Troy, who sat on the sofa, she paused. "Hi."

Troy rose from his seat, and their gazes met and clung. Sadie remembered every vivid detail of kissing him the night before, knowing he was losing control and luxuriating in the knowledge that he wanted her. From the expression in his eyes, she could see he was remembering, too, but he quickly looked away, impersonally facing the woman who sat in the over-stuffed chair.

"Sadie, this is Frannie White."

As Troy said her name, Frannie rose and extended her hand to shake Sadie's. Though tall and athletic, she still managed to look feminine. Her red hair was cut in a cute, bouncy style. Her trendy short shirt and jeans made her look like a teenager.

"I'm considering hiring her to be the girls' body-guard."

Sadie shook Frannie's hand. "It's nice to meet you."

Troy motioned for Sadie to sit on the sofa and sat beside her, though he kept his distance. "I think a female bodyguard for the girls is long overdue," he said then glanced at Bruce, who hadn't left the room as Sadie had thought, but lounged against the door frame. "Right, Bruce?"

Bruce smiled and shrugged nonchalantly. "Right."

Frannie chuckled. "Actually, it is," she said. "Ms. Evans, Mr. Cramer has explained that you've been helping the girls, and I thought you and I should talk so that I could get a better understanding of them."

"And also so that you can form an honest opinion about whether or not Frannie would be a good choice for the girls."

Sadie turned and gaped at Troy. "In other words, if I don't like Frannie she will be fired?"

"She isn't hired yet. All of this is preliminary. If you don't think she's a good match for the girls, we'll find somebody who is."

"Being a bodyguard is a very personal thing, Ms. Evans," Frannie said, adding to Troy's explanation. "I don't want to be hired to guard someone who won't take my instructions because they don't like me. I also wouldn't want to be hired for someone who isn't a good fit for me, somebody—or in this case, two people—whose lives would be in jeopardy because I didn't understand them.''

Sadie smiled and nodded, but she knew why Troy had brought her in on this discussion. He was reinforcing what he had told her last night. His life was unusual and difficult. He was showing her it wasn't her fault she couldn't fit in. Few people could. She suspected he meant to comfort her, but proving she didn't fit into his world simply intensified the hurt of knowing she and Troy could never be together.

Frannie leaned forward. ''Can I make a suggestion?''

From his position at the doorway, Bruce said, ''That's what you're here for.''

''Let me get acquainted with your household, with the twins and with you, Sadie,'' Frannie said, nodding toward Sadie. ''You'll see how I work. You can watch me with the girls.'' She shrugged. ''And you'll get a clear picture of whether or not I'm a good fit for them.''

Sadie cautiously glanced at Troy, not wanting to stir up her feelings for him again yet knowing that as long as she worked for him she had to communicate with him. ''How does that sound to you?''

''Perfect,'' Troy said. Nonchalant and cool, he held her gaze, and Sadie realized that the more time they spent together the more detached he would make himself and the more it would hurt her. ''That way if Frannie works, we're actually easing into this already.''

''Okay.''

"Okay."

Frannie rose. "I understand the girls swim in the morning."

Troy and Sadie rose, too. "Yes."

"Do you want me to swim? Would you like me to stand on the perimeter? What would *you* like, Sadie?"

"I would like private time with the girls to explain the change to them. I would also like to help them get to know you and accept you, since having a female bodyguard is going to be very different. Even if you don't take the job, I think the girls need to be told the change will eventually be made."

Troy said, "I'll come with you when you tell them."

Sadie faced him. "Really?" Though Troy was definitely pulling away from her, he seemed to have finally caught on. If nothing else, Sadie knew she had accomplished the biggest part of what needed to be done for Troy and his girls. She had shown Troy that he needed to be more directly involved in his daughters' lives, and he had taken her advice.

"Yes," he began, but Bruce interrupted him.

"Boss, if there's nothing else I think Frannie and I will shuffle on out of here. I'll familiarize her with the grounds."

"Okay."

Frannie and Bruce left the room and headed for the kitchen. Sadie faced Troy again. "You're learning."

He nodded. "Yes. You kept saying the girls need more contact with me, and I finally saw that the best contact I can have is to be the one who explains things to them. That makes me the law."

Studying his face, which had become so dear to her, Sadie smiled. "As far as the girls are concerned, you need to be the law. So I'm not going to be the one to tell them about Frannie. You can. I'll just be backup."

She began to walk to the door, but Troy caught her hand. "There's just one more thing."

Knowing she had to keep her composure around him and that she couldn't react to the fact that he so casually grabbed her hand, Sadie coolly turned and said, "Yes?"

"I'm sorry about last night."

She could see from the expression in his eyes that he was sorry. He was very sorry. But he wasn't going to change his mind. Sadie did not belong in his world, and that was all there was to it. It didn't matter if she kissed him, if he wanted her. Facts were facts, and people like Troy didn't try to bend or twist them.

A spasm of pain shivered through her, but she forced a smile. "Don't worry about it. I was just overwhelmed with concern for you. Your life is hard."

"I'm glad you see that."

"Oh, yes," she said, feigning a confidence she didn't feel. "It was stupid of me not to realize it before."

"So, we're good then?"

"Absolutely."

"Friends?"

Pain squeezed her heart, and she told him the one thing she was certain of about this relationship. "We'll always be friends."

"Okay." He directed her out of the living room and to the spiral stairway in the foyer. "So what are you and the girls going to do today?"

"After we swim this morning, I'm taking them to the day care."

Troy stopped on the step. "You are?"

"Yes. Troy, they really like it. In fact, I was going to recommend that we enroll them."

"Enroll them?"

"For the opportunity to spend time with other kids, play organized games, have at least some part of their day that's normal."

Troy blew his breath out on a long sigh. "Okay. No problem. But if this is going to be permanent, that means certain arrangements have to be made." He drew a quick breath. "Plus, with Frannie in the picture but not yet trained, you'll have to take two bodyguards instead of one."

Sadie shrugged. "That's okay. You should see the way Bruce blends. No one would ever know he wasn't one of the day-care workers. Besides, having a few extra adults is a plus at a day care. I'll call Caro and let her knew we're coming."

Troy shook his head. "*I'll* call Caro."

Sadie stopped walking and looked at him. "Really?"

"Yes. I told you. I now understand what you've been trying to teach me all along. I need to be more involved in the girls' lives."

"Well, good," Sadie said, almost euphoric that this had sunk in. "Call Caro. Tell her what you want, and I'm sure she'll have my parents accommodate you," Sadie said, but seeing how much he had changed sent the oddest surge of feelings through her. His dedication to doing the right thing made her proud of him, and love for him overwhelmed her. Yet she knew she couldn't have him, which made her love for him painful. Worse, because he wanted to be actively involved in the girls' lives, they would spend more time together in her final week of working for him. She would work with him, loving him, seeing all his wonderful changes, and not really be a part of it.

By the time Sadie, Rosemary, Ginger, Frannie and Bruce arrived at the day care, Troy had called. Though an ordinary observer might not have noticed anything amiss, it was clear to Sadie that Troy had given her sister Caro specific instructions on how the girls were to be treated.

"Hi, Rosemary, Ginger," Sadie's dad said as he guided them up the steps. "I understand you're going to be with us for a few weeks."

Ginger blinked at him. "Sadie said we're coming here every day until school starts."

"Yes, you are," Lilly confirmed from her rocker in the middle of the big playroom. "I have Jack," she added.

Ginger's eyes widened dramatically, and she pivoted and raced across the room. "Hi, Jack!"

Jack pulled his mouth away from the bottle Sadie's mother held for him and gurgled with delight.

"Would you like to spend the morning in here, helping again?" Lilly asked.

"Yeah!"

"And, Rosie, you and I can go outside and play with the other kids if you like," Bruce said, pointing out the window.

"You mean it?" Rosemary asked Bruce, and her voice was so filled with awe that Sadie's eyes misted.

"He means it," Sadie said.

"Grab the Wiffle ball equipment," Sadie's father said to Bruce, "and let's go outside."

"Okay," Bruce said, sounding almost as happy as

Rosemary. "Frannie, you're with us. Sadie takes care of inside duty."

When they left, Caro walked to Sadie. With her brown eyes and blond hair, Sadie's little sister was a younger version of their mother. "So, these are the infamous bad twins."

Sadie nodded. "Yep."

"They don't look bad."

"They aren't. Not really. They're just confused because they've been raised in a household of men." She caught Caro's gaze. "But now that Frannie will be with them, things will change considerably."

Caro said. "Good." At the same time, the door opened, and Caro's fiancé, Max Riley, stepped inside, toting his daughter, Bethany, in her baby seat.

Caro dropped everything and walked to the door to greet them. "Hi!"

Tall and athletic, with dark hair and blue eyes, Max gave Caro a quick kiss. "Hi." Peering around Caro, he saw Sadie and said, "Hi, Sadie. What brings you here?"

"She's here with Troy Cramer's twins," Caro said, taking the baby carrier from Max and setting it on the table to lift Bethany out. The little girl wasn't yet a year old. Bethany, half-asleep, cuddled against Caro's shoulder.

Something tugged at Sadie's heartstrings. She knew Caro would be a good mother. She looked so perfect, so natural, so ethereal. Seeing her in the role almost brought tears to Sadie's eyes.

"You're very good with her," Sadie commented, walking to where Max and Caro stood.

Caro laughed. "I do work at a day care."

Sadie smiled. "Yeah. That gives you an edge."

"I don't have an edge," Caro said, taking Bethany to a rocker. "All the Evanses are good with kids."

"Yeah. I think you're proof of that, Sadie," Max agreed, leaning against a changing table. "I haven't seen you with the Cramer twins, but your mother says you're a marvel with them."

This time Sadie's eyes did fill with tears. "Really? She said that?"

"Yeah," Caro said, snuggling Bethany closer. "She said the first day the girls visited they were awkward, but before the afternoon was over, she didn't just see improvement in their behavior, she also saw that they liked and respected you."

At Caro's words, Sadie began to cry.

Max pushed away from the table. Caro said, "Sadie?"

Sadie waved her hand in dismissal. "It's nothing."

"It's something," Max said, walking to her and looking into her face. "I've never seen you cry," he said, putting his arm around her shoulders to comfort her. "Which means whatever has you crying is important. So spill it. What's up?"

"I... I..." She couldn't finish. She couldn't say, "I love the twins." It hurt too much. And that was the problem. Every day she worked with Ginger and Rosemary she got closer to them. Every day, they got closer to her. When Sadie stopped visiting, they would miss her, and she would ache for them.

She burst into tears. "I can't do this anymore."

Caro frowned. "Do what?"

"I can't play mother to twins I'm going to lose in a week—two if I'm lucky." Realizing that was the truth, and that she had to do something about it, she drew a quick breath. "I think I need to go have a talk with Troy."

Caro and Max exchanged a glance. Max said, "Caro, what's going on?"

Knowing she had to talk about at least some of this, Sadie sighed. "Troy and I skirted around a personal relationship and decided against it."

Max studied her face. "It looks to me like he decided alone, since you're not too happy about it."

"I'm not happy about it, but I understand his decision."

"But?" Max prompted.

"But I suddenly see that though he could decide against the relationship, and I had to agree with his reasoning, he can't call all the shots."

Caro said, "You really like him, don't you?"

Sadie nodded. "And the twins. And it suddenly seems incredibly stupid to stay there when all it's going to do is hurt me."

Max frowned. "Don't you still have things to teach the twins?"

Sadie shook her head. "No. The twins' problem was that Troy didn't get involved enough in their lives, and this morning he proved to me that he understands what he needs to do. There's no reason for me to work for him anymore." She paused, took a long breath. "So, if you two wouldn't mind, I would like to go talk with him now. Can I leave the twins with you until I get back?"

"Hey, Sadie, this is a day care," Caro said. "By rights you should be able to drop off the girls and go. Instead, you stay and you bring bodyguards."

Max laughed. "Yeah, Sadie. Look around. This

protection Troy insists on is starting to feel like over-kill.''

"He doesn't think so," Sadie said, but she under-stood what Max and Caro were saying. Troy's insis-tence on extra people was a burden on the day care. "I'm going to have to borrow your car because Bruce drove me here."

Max tossed his keys to her. "Use mine."

When Sadie arrived at the estate everything was quiet. Joe the gardener buzzed her in, and Jake met her at the front door, concern etched on his face.

"What's up? Where are the twins?"

"I left them at the day care with Bruce and Frannie because I need to talk to Troy."

Jake studied her. Sadie tried to look cool and un-affected, and for a few seconds she was convinced she had pulled it off, but Jake's expression softened. He stepped away from the door and invited her inside.

"He's on a conference call right now, but you can go back to his office to wait." He turned toward the kitchen. "Sometimes when he gets these long confer-ence calls I go make a sandwich. I'll be here for a good half hour," he continued, not looking at Sadie, but letting her know he was giving her privacy. "So whatever it is you want to say, you take your time."

With that he left, and Sadie drew a long breath. Well, she knew what she had to do, and she now had the privacy to do it. She took another breath and headed down the hall.

When she stepped inside Troy's office he was stand-ing, staring out the window, not talking on the phone. She cleared her throat. "Hey."

Troy turned from the window. "Hey," he said, sounding confused. "Where are the girls?"

"With Bruce, Frannie, my mom, my dad, my sister Caro and her fiancé, Max Riley, at the day care. They're in good hands."

Troy grimaced. "Right."

"Lots of good hands."

This time Troy chuckled. "I get it, Sadie."

"I don't think you do," Sadie said, knowing the moment of truth was at hand. "If I thought it was my place I might mention that you have the girls a tad overprotected." Troy bristled, but Sadie didn't give him a chance to talk. "But it's not my place, and that's actually why I'm here."

He motioned for her to take a seat, indicating with his movement that she should also keep talking.

She drew a long, fortifying breath. "I think it's time for me to bow out."

He sat on the chair behind his desk. "Bow out?"

"Yeah."

"You can't bow out. Our deal extends until the first day of school. Though technically you have only another week, we agreed that you would be available for that third week before classes start." He paused and caught her gaze. "I need you."

Sadie swallowed hard. "Troy, you don't need me. You have Frannie now."

"The girls don't know her well enough for her to step into your shoes."

"Then let me put it this way, Troy." She squeezed her eyes shut. "I can't do this anymore."

Troy looked at her drawn face and without explanation he understood what she was saying. Being around each other, having feelings that seemed to grow by leaps and bounds every day, feelings they couldn't do anything about, was the most difficult thing he had ever done.

He tapped his pencil on his desk and blew his breath out on a sigh. "I know how hard it is."

She opened her eyes and looked at him. "Do you?"

He nodded. "Yes. Do you think it's easy for me to be around you all the time?"

"This is different, Troy. Though it hurts me to be around you and know we can't ever be anything to one another, being around the girls is worse. They're bringing out something in me that could change me permanently. If I don't leave soon I'm going to feel so much like their mother that leaving them will be the hardest thing I've ever done."

Troy's heart squeezed. Knowing that Sadie loved his daughters was equal parts pleasure and pain. He wished she could be their mother. He wished it with all his heart. But she couldn't.

He also understood the other side of her dilemma. He loved his daughters with an intensity that shocked him. He knew that if someone told him he had only two weeks before they would be taken away, it would kill him. He couldn't imagine the torment Sadie was suffering.

"Okay," he said, then swallowed hard. "I'm going to let you out of our deal."

"I'm sorry."

"It's okay. Because I have a few conditions."

She nodded.

"First, I can't let you out today. I would like for you to stay one more day so you can take me to the day care tomorrow, familiarize me with everything that goes on there and the girls' daily rituals. That way I can be the liaison with Frannie.''

Sadie smiled sadly. ''You're the one who should be doing it anyway.''

''Right,'' Troy agreed, smiling bitterly. He finally caught on to what needed to be done. He finally pleased her. And she was leaving, pushed out because his life was too darned difficult for anyone to handle. ''And I'll still pay your aunt the one hundred thousand dollars.''

''Oh, Troy, we can't hold you to that.''

Troy caught her gaze. ''You did exactly what I needed, Sadie. You turned my little girls into little girls again. I can't thank you enough.'' *And I can't tell you how much I'll miss you.* He almost said it. He almost voiced all the sorrow in his heart at being trapped in his life. But he didn't. He wouldn't burden her with the pain of knowing how excruciating this was for him.

Sadie rose. ''I'll come back tomorrow, and we'll go to the day care together.''

''Right,'' Troy said, also rising.

She valiantly put out her hand to shake his, and he took it. He allowed himself to memorize her soft skin. He let himself gaze into her wonderful eyes. He let his heart feel everything he wanted to feel but wasn't allowed. He tucked the memories away, knowing he would need them when she was gone. Then he released her hand.

''I'll see you tomorrow.''

Chapter Nine

Walking up to Troy's front door the next morning, Sadie took a gulp of air. This would all be over soon, and she could get on with the rest of her life. So her heart wasn't supposed to beat faster in anticipation of seeing him. She wasn't supposed to get breathless and excited. Her reaction proved that when this job was finished, she was going to be hurt. She had to do everything in her power to break the ties today, or she would never get over losing Troy and the girls.

She opened the door without ringing the bell and sneaked upstairs to get the twins without Troy noticing. Once the girls were ready for the morning at day care, she explained to Troy that she would take her own car, since there was no point in her returning to his house after they were done at the day care. Though his jaw twitched, he agreed. Then he jumped into his little blue convertible, and Bruce drove the twins and Frannie in the van.

When they arrived, the girls hopped out of the van

and, without waiting for Bruce, ran to the front gate to be buzzed in. Sadie saw Troy stiffen. "They do this all the time?"

"What?"

"Get out of the van without help?"

"It's called walking, Troy. The girls seem to like it."

Troy caught her hand to keep her from getting close enough to the twins that they could hear the discussion. "I wasn't talking about walking, I was talking about getting away from Bruce."

"They aren't that far away. Besides, when they are in school they have to be completely away from him. He's probably not permitted to go into a classroom. And you wouldn't want him to be in the classrooms. You want them to behave normally."

Troy glanced around. "I want them to be safe."

"Look at the yard, Troy. There's a six-foot fence."

He nodded.

"And the yard is full of kids. Nobody in his right mind would try to grab or hurt one of these kids. Too many witnesses. Too many obstacles to overcome before you reach them."

"You really believe that?"

Sadie nodded. "Yes. As a police officer I believe that. Frankly, by always having a bodyguard with your kids you might be calling undue attention to them."

Troy looked around again. "It does seem that way."

"Because it's true. And since you're in the mood to make concessions, think about this one. We're bringing you, me, Frannie and Bruce to an already crowded backyard."

Troy peered at the kids inside the fence. There had

to be twenty of them, plus Sadie's dad and a woman who looked about twenty. "And?"

"And I think we should ask Bruce to go home for a while." She paused and smiled hopefully. "At least until you're done inspecting the place. When you're ready to leave, he can return."

Troy examined the scene one more time. If there really was safety in numbers, his daughters couldn't be any more protected. "Okay. Except I want to reverse it. Bruce stays. Frannie leaves. When I'm done here then Frannie can return."

"Whatever you want."

Troy walked to Frannie and instructed her to return to the estate. But he remembered Sadie saying Bruce called attention to the girls. Looking around, seeing the kids and adults, Troy had to admit big, muscular Bruce did look out of place. For the first time Troy recognized he really could be calling attention to his kids, which wouldn't protect them but mark them as the targets.

Still, with his daughters' bodyguard situation in flux, today wasn't the day to do anything about it. Frannie acknowledged Troy's direction to leave and ambled off to the van.

Troy joined Sadie at the fence. She pushed a button and said, "Hey, Mom, it's me."

The fence buzzed, indicating that the gate could be opened, and Troy faced Sadie. "The day care has security?"

Sadie looked at him as if he were crazy. "Of course! In the summer there are sometimes as many as fifty kids here. We don't want anybody getting in or out without us knowing."

"Right. Good idea," Troy agreed, struck by a new

thought. Sadie was accustomed to security. Which meant she wasn't as opposed to it as she seemed to think she was. For the first time since he began to have romantic feelings for her, he suddenly saw that though they were on opposite ends of the spectrum, they nonetheless shared the basic knowledge that some people had to be protected. But more than that, when she was in the day care, Sadie accepted the limits of the precaution.

Sadie led him up the stairs of the back porch and into a little room that had hooks for coats and cubbyholes.

Sadie's mother greeted them the second they stepped through the door. "Hi!"

"You remember Troy Cramer, right, Mom?"

"Of course," she said, smiling warmly. "We met Troy when he made arrangements to hire you, Sadie." She turned to Sadie's father, who was approaching them. "I'm sure he remembers your dad."

"Troy," Pete Evans said, extending his hand to shake Troy's. "Sadie tells us you want to spend some time with us."

Troy laughed. "I heard my daughters did chores here. I wanted to see it."

Lilly laughed and pointed to the right. Sure enough, Ginger was stacking disposable diapers on a shelf beside a changing table.

"And over there," Pete said, directing Troy's attention to where Rosemary was digging through a toy bin.

"What's she doing?"

"She has a favorite ball."

Troy's eyes misted unexpectedly. "A favorite ball?"

"She hit two home runs when she was here yesterday and she's convinced it's because of the ball." Pete faced Troy with a smile. "Now that we know the girls will be coming here every day, next week we can switch balls without telling her, wait until she hits another home run, then tell her it's her talent getting the hits, not the ball."

Pride and emotion welled in Troy's chest. "This is so good for them."

"Having peers is good for everybody," Lilly said. "And so is competition. That's what shapes their personalities."

Troy remembered that Sadie had suggested he send his daughters to Wilburn Elementary, and suddenly he understood why. Here they were part of a community. Part of *their* community, because Wilburn was the town they lived in. He saw the progress the day care had made in a few visits. He understood what Sadie was telling him.

"So far I like what I see."

"Why don't you come outside and play ball with us?" Pete suggested as Rosemary approached, carrying two bats and her favorite ball.

"Yeah, Dad!" she said, her eyes wide and bright with excitement.

He ruffled her hair. "Okay."

"I'll stay in here with Ginger," Sadie said. "And you can take Bruce outside with you guys. He can umpire."

"Umpire?" Bruce asked, moving closer. "The last two times I was team captain!"

"Then why don't you play and I'll umpire," Troy suggested.

"Not on your life, nerd boy," Sadie said with a

laugh. "My mother and I want to watch from the window."

Troy laughed. "I'm not exactly the incompetent I was in grade school."

She smiled at him, and conflicting thoughts buffeted Troy. She was so beautiful and she made him so happy that he would love to have her in his life, if only to see that smile every day.

She caught his gaze. "I'm counting on it."

As Troy stared into her pretty green eyes, all his defenses fell away. He wanted her. He wanted her in his life more than he had ever wanted anything. His thoughts melded into one solid conclusion. If she was right, if he was overprotecting everybody, then he could bring her into his life.

Unable to believe he had had that thought, Troy shook his head. A compromise was a wonderfully convenient thing. Particularly since the deal would deliver Sadie to his waiting arms. He couldn't jeopardize his daughters' lives because of a beautiful woman.

He brought himself back to the present and said, "Just for that, I'm team captain, and I'm going to whip your dad's team."

Bruce hooted with excitement. "All right! A real game. And the ump is the guy with the power. Let's go!"

"Wait one second," Lilly said, walking away. She stopped at the changing table where Ginger was checking bottles of lotion and containers of powder to be sure they had adequate supplies. "Honey, your dad is going to play ball this morning. If you want, you can go, too."

"I have two more bottles to check."

"I'll—" Sadie began but her mother stopped her with a look and turned to Ginger.

"That will take you two minutes. You finish up while your dad and Mr. Evans pick sides. By the time you're done they'll be ready for you."

Ginger's eyes brightened. "Okay."

Troy felt another unexpected jolt of emotion. He'd never seen Ginger so polite or so normal. No, he'd never seen Ginger so happy. And it was all because Sadie had skirted the rules. She'd brought his twins to the outside world without his permission. And they hadn't been hurt. They had been helped.

He didn't get the chance to dwell on it. Within seconds, he was swept outside to choose sides for a Wiffle ball game. Given his athletic history, he didn't shy away from the smart kid, the chubby kid or the skinny little girl. In fact, he put all of them on his team.

"So everything they say about you is true," Pete commented when the sides were chosen and Ginger came running down the stairs to join them.

"What?"

"You're not just smart. You're crafty."

Troy laughed. "You got that from the way I picked a Wiffle ball team?"

"We both know brute strength doesn't count for squat in Wiffle ball. Sometimes a weak swing will take an airy plastic ball a lot farther. I see who you picked. You chose the kids who won't swing hard. You're probably going to whip the tar out of us."

"I am a genius."

Pete laughed, and Bruce offered a quarter for a coin toss to see who was up first. Pete's team won the toss, and Troy's took the outfield. Troy quickly learned that brute strength may not help a team at bat, but it would be nice to have a kid who could throw the ball. By the time Pete's side retired, they had thirty runs.

"Not a problem," Troy said, clapping his hands to gather his team. "We'll catch them."

Johnny Jeffries pushed his glasses up his nose. "I don't think so, Mr. Cramer. With only three possible mistake opportunities in the form of outs, the odds of us getting thirty runs before the other team stops three of our players aren't very good."

Troy burst out laughing. "So this is what I sounded like?"

Sadie grimaced as she brought a pitcher of lemonade and glasses to one of the redwood picnic tables. "Yes."

"Well, then, I think I was adorable."

"You're still adorable."

She said it casually, but Troy's heart leaped to his throat. She really liked him. Not his money, certainly not his lifestyle, not the idea of being his wife. She liked *him*. Sometimes the notion blew him away. What she offered was simple and wonderful. A friend. A companion. Someone who liked him as well as loved him. Exactly what he wanted. Exactly what he *needed*. And he knew he wouldn't be much of a genius if he let her get away.

At bat, Troy's team managed to get twenty-six runs. Though still down by four, they hooted and hollered their way to the outfield. Smarter this time, Troy's team only gave up five runs. But Pete's team also wised up about their fielding, and they only gave up five runs. The close game went on for another two innings. Tired and thirsty, Troy suggested they take a break.

Sadie laughed at him. "You need a regular exercise routine."

"I play tennis every morning," he assured her, rolling his eyes as he made his way to a cooler of water Sadie had placed next to the lemonade.

"There are cookies here, too!" she called, and the kids descended on them like starving wolves.

Sadie laughed. "Help yourself to a cookie, Bruce, before they're all gone!"

"Yeah, Bruce," Troy said.

Bruce's cell phone rang. He slid it from his jeans pocket, pressed it to his ear and shifted away from the picnic table.

"The girls love this," Troy began. He wasn't sure what else to say. He didn't want to give Sadie false hope by telling her he finally found a compromise position that might allow them to have a relationship before he really thought things through. Because this was not a simple matter. Not only were his daughters' lives at stake, but he didn't want to break Sadie's heart if it didn't work. He didn't want to get his own heart broken. Though the compromise seemed right, it also seemed too easy. At the same time it seemed too drastic.

Bruce suddenly turned to Troy and Sadie.

"My father's had a heart attack."

Sadie gasped. "Oh, my gosh, I'm so sorry!"

Wide-eyed and confused, typically controlled Bruce said, "I have to get to Missouri."

Without thinking Troy said, "Nigel will fly you there." He pulled his keys from his jeans pocket. "Take my car back to the house. I'll call Joe and tell him to make arrangements for the plane and to drive you to the airstrip."

Bruce nodded, took Troy's keys and ran out the gate. Troy called Joe, gave him instructions and added that Joe should send Frannie to the day care.

"I hope he's all right," Sadie said.

"Me, too," Troy said, shoving down the antenna of his cell phone.

"That was pretty darned nice of you."

"And it's also one of those perks I was telling you about. I can do a lot of things for my friends, my family and my employees that a normal man can't."

Before Sadie could answer Pete yelled, "Okay. Let's play ball!"

Troy tossed his paper cup into a trash can. "Play ball!" he called, gathering his team, who took the outfield. They played an entire inning before Troy realized he and his daughters were in public without a bodyguard.

He froze, not sure what to do. Then the Wiffle ball hit him square on the head, and on instinct he reached down, grabbed it and tossed it to first base. Rosemary expertly caught it, tagging the runner out.

"Good job, Rosemary!"

"Thanks, Dad!" she said, and before Troy had a chance to say anything to anyone about a bodyguard, Pete Evans had another player at the plate. Todd Nelson, pitcher for Troy's team, wound up and tossed the ball.

Strike one.

Troy almost called time-out, but he glanced around. Surely Frannie would arrive any second.

Strike two.

And no good team captain wanted to call time-out when his pitcher was clearly hot.

Strike three.

"Okay, Todd!" he yelled, instinct taking over. The day was bright and sunny. The neighborhood was quiet. The kids were having fun. *His* kids were having fun. Damn it! *He* was having fun.

He was having fun.

He was quietly, unexpectedly free.

And he liked it.

And he understood why his girls were slowly being driven to badness.

And he knew beyond a shadow of a doubt he had gone overboard.

Two weeks later Sadie entered the diner to find Troy and Jake seated at a booth. She had been miserable without him, and she knew talking to him would only put her back to the beginning of getting over him, but she couldn't resist.

As she approached the table, she expected Jake's broad smile, but Troy's beaming face was a complete surprise. He looked like the happiest man in the world. While she had been miserable without him, he appeared to have been very happy without her.

She stopped. "What are you doing here?"

Both Troy and Jake quickly looked up. Jake said, "Hi, Sadie!"

But Troy sucked in his breath at the sight of her. Even in her police uniform, she was beautiful. He had longed for her every minute of the two weeks they had spent apart, but he hadn't called her because he wasn't ready. Seeing her today, he realized it was time. Everything in his life was in place. Everything was working. He had made all his compromises. Now he had to ask her to make hers.

Jake said, "We're finishing lunch, but you can join us for a minute or two if you want."

Troy fought to keep himself from jumping out of the booth and forcing her to sit down. As calmly as possible, he said, "Yes, join us."

"No, I'm here to pick up take-out orders. I can't stay." She faced Troy and caught his gaze. "It's just very odd to see you here…in public like this."

"We come here for lunch almost every day now," Jake said. "Troy's changing his life."

With his gaze locked on hers, Troy said, "Yes. I am. I've actually done a lot of things. Things you suggested."

She gave him a confused look. "Really?"

"For one, the girls have been enrolled in Wilburn Elementary."

She stared at him. "That's great."

Troy laughed, but nervousness filled him. He had lightened his security. He had enrolled his girls in the local elementary school. He and the girls were integrating into the community. Partly because it was good for the girls, and partly because he wanted a shot with Sadie. He had proved to himself that he could pare down and still be safe, and for the past two weeks he had been living a nearly normal life. Now came the hard part.

He took a quick breath, ready to ask her out, but Charlotte ambled over with a brown paper bag. "I assume you're here for these, Sadie Belle."

Sadie turned and smiled at Charlotte. "Yeah. I'll be up to the register in a second."

Charlotte winked at Sadie, then at Troy, and as far as Troy was concerned, it was official. They were now an item. This time tomorrow the entire town would know they had talked. This time next week there would be a betting pool for people to guess their wedding date. He might as well ask Sadie out.

When Charlotte walked away, Jake burst out laughing. "Oh, you two are in trouble. You are now in the diner rumor mill. I would bet you take the number-one spot as Charlotte's gossip of the day as soon as we walk out the door."

Sadie sighed. "Who cares?"

Jake stretched, then rose from the booth. "Well, while you two are talking, I'm going to pay my bill. I'll meet you in the SUV."

Sadie said, "I better go, too."

But Troy caught her arm to keep her from leaving. The usual lightning bolt flashed through him, and he knew he was doing the right thing. When Jake was at the cash register, Troy said, "I was wondering if you would come out to the house tonight."

One of her perfect black eyebrows arched. "Trouble with the girls?"

"No, they're fine. Wonderful. But I know they would love to see you."

"Oh."

He caught her gaze. Held it. Counted on the fact that she would see a hundred times more in his eyes than most people saw. "I would love to see you, too."

She studied his face for a second then smiled slowly. "Really?"

"More than you would ever know."

Sadie saw the serious expression in his eyes and believed him. But she knew there was more to this decision than the fact that he missed her. First, there was the matter of his lifestyle. Second, he had never said he loved her. She fell for him in a matter of days.

He didn't have those kinds of feelings. If she got involved with him and he never developed those feelings, her heart would be shattered.

Her smile faded, and she swallowed. "I don't know. I don't want to reopen old wounds, Troy. I loved those little girls and..."

He placed a finger over her lips. "I changed my life because you are right. I need somebody to share my life."

Sadie licked her suddenly dry lips. He said, *need somebody to share*. Not *love*.

"But I couldn't bring another person into a land of bodyguards and supertight security. I didn't think it was fair. So I changed." He paused and drew a deep breath. "I changed for you. Because I like you."

She swallowed. Like was much better than need. It gave her hope. "Then I'll be by at eight."

Sadie arrived at Troy's house that night, and the girls met her at the door. They were dressed in T-shirts and denim shorts and it was hard to believe they had ever had a penchant for snakeskin and feather boas.

"Hi, Ginger," she said hugging the first twin. "And Rosemary," she said as she hugged the second.

"We go to school here now."

"We have our friends over."

"Frannie taught us to play football."

"I'm trying out for cheerleader when we get into sixth grade."

Sadie listened to the barrage of comments, saying, "Really," every couple of seconds. The girls chattered nonstop as they led her to the patio. Hardly pausing for air, they sat around the umbrella table and talked

about school and how much fun it was to have friends
and play volleyball and take a real gym class.

Sadie watched Troy sit back and let the girls giggle
and talk and show Sadie schoolwork they dredged
from book bags they had left in the hall.

When it was a little after nine, Frannie walked out
to the patio. "You have about fifteen minutes to
shower before lights out."

The faces of both girls fell. Both said, "Aw!"

Troy said, "Don't worry. Sadie will be back."

The twins faced their dad. "She will?"

Sadie caught Troy's gaze. "I will?"

Troy smiled. "Sure, Sadie can visit any time she
likes."

"Will you?" Rosemary asked.

Knowing that Troy was telling her he had fulfilled
his part of the bargain and the ball was in her court,
Sadie carefully considered before she spoke. "I would
like to, but your dad and I have some things to talk
about before I can make the promise."

"Dad?"

He held his hands up. "Hey, what Sadie and I have
to discuss is between us. You two don't get a vote.
And you're also not going to browbeat me into seeing
things your way. Go with Frannie."

Frannie put her hands on the girls' shoulders and
turned them toward the French doors.

Ginger ducked out from under Frannie's hold. She
raced to Sadie and gave her a hug before quickly running back to the bodyguard-turned-nanny.

"That's one, Ginger," Frannie said, clearly exasperated as she turned her toward the French door
again.

But Ginger only giggled and waved, making Sadie laugh.

When they were gone, Sadie became nervous. In her heart she knew she had been waiting all her adult life for Troy. But she also knew she couldn't push him. He had done a lot of changing, but he had mentioned that she would have to compromise, too. With the moment of truth at hand, and with her desperate need to hear him say he had missed her as much as she had missed him, she couldn't stand the thought that he might ask for something she couldn't do.

"I understand we were the object of this afternoon's gossip in town."

Sadie smiled slightly. "Sorry about that. I shouldn't have stopped at your table."

"I haven't just changed how I feel about protection and bodyguards. I've changed a lot of things lately. The gossip doesn't bother me, either."

"Good. And I can see the changes," Sadie said, glad to keep the casual conversation going because she was so nervous. "Frannie acts more like a nanny than a bodyguard."

Troy nodded. "Bruce is still head of security, but he doesn't cook anymore."

Sadie laughed. "That's a pity. That man makes a mean spaghetti sauce."

Several seconds passed in silence before Troy said, "Even though everything was changing we all noticed you were gone. We all missed you."

Sadie swallowed the lump in her throat. "I missed you guys, too."

"You said you were growing attached to the girls. I knew you would miss them."

Sadie drew a long breath, gathered all her courage

and caught his gaze. "I didn't just miss the girls. I missed *you*, too."

"I missed you, too. A lot."

He rose and put his hand on the back of Sadie's chair, helping her to stand. "Walk with me?"

"Sure."

They got as far as a garden ten feet beyond the pool before he stopped. He looped his arms around her waist and pulled her close.

"I can't promise you anything—"

Sadie interrupted him with a laugh. "Troy, it looks like you could promise a woman everything."

He shook his head. "I'm not talking about material things. When it comes to material things, I could buy you your own country." He paused and drew a long breath. "Sadie, I really like you."

Totally unprepared for the seriousness of his tone, Sadie gaped at him. "You're not going to propose, are you?"

He shook his head. "I'm not ready for that, but I want you to know that when I ask you to the movies I don't take it lightly."

Not sure how to respond, Sadie laughed. "You don't take anything lightly, Troy."

"So, you'll come to a movie with me?"

She peered at him. "By movie you don't mean private screening at Steven Spielberg's house, do you?"

He laughed. "Not this time."

"Then I would love to go to the movies with you."

"Really?"

"Really."

He kissed her then, and Sadie genuinely believed everything was going to be okay. She absolutely adored him, and he didn't love her. Yet. But that was the whole point in dating someone. Eventually he would love her.

She hoped.

Chapter Ten

Comfortable, happy for the first time in almost two years, Troy stood by his office window. Watching his daughters swim with four of their newfound buddies, he realized in the two weeks that had passed since his visit to the day care, his life had changed completely. And now he and Sadie were going on a date. A real date. And his daughters had made friends. They had visited the homes of those friends without accompaniment. And nothing had gone wrong.

Though Bruce and Joe still hovered at the pool, they acted more as lifeguards than bodyguards. Low key. Quiet. They were seated close enough to solve a problem should one arise, but not so close that they interrupted the fun. They could have been invisible for all his twins and their friends noticed.

Girlish giggles and squeals filled the air, and as Troy watched and listened, joy filled him. He had never believed his life could feel this good again.

"Troy, you have a call on line four."

He turned and smiled when Joni burst into his office. "Would you look at them?" he said with a laugh then nodded beyond the window to the pool. "I've never seen them so happy!"

"Troy! You have a call on line four! It's Sadie's dad. It's urgent!"

"Nothing is urgent anymore, Joni—"

"This is," she said, and for the first time Troy noticed her eyes were filled with tears, and her hands were shaking. "Sadie was in an accident."

He grabbed the telephone as Jake came running into the room. "So what do we do?"

Joni caught his hand. "Troy's just picking up the call now."

Troy didn't have to talk to Sadie's dad to know what he was going to hear. It felt like two years ago all over again. The people were different. The office was different. But the situation was the same. He could feel it in the ice that flowed through his blood, freezing his muscles, and the fear that paralyzed his brain.

"Pete?"

"Troy, I'm sorry. Sadie's been in an accident...."

Troy's chest muscles tightened. His limbs went numb. He knew Pete's dulled, disbelieving tone of voice too well.

"And she's hurt," Troy said, unable to let himself think any further than that. He couldn't let himself imagine the worst. That she was dead. But in his gut he knew she was.

Just like Angelina.

"Yes, she was hurt pretty badly."

"How badly?" he asked, his voice tight and drawn. Doctors would work to save her and fail. A solemn-faced surgeon would meet him in the waiting room and tell him they had tried everything. And Troy's whole world would crumble at his feet.

Again.

"We're at the hospital now."

"Which hospital?"

"University."

"I'll be there in twenty minutes." He didn't say goodbye, simply cradled the receiver. Then he spent a few seconds working to pull his emotions in line before he said anything or looked at anyone. When he was ready, he glanced at Jake. "Call Nigel. I need him to fly me to the hospital. Tell him there's no time to waste and that he should make the arrangements to land on the hospital heliport on his way to the hanger." He faced Joni. "Can you stay with the girls?"

Pressing her lips together, she nodded mutely.

Troy ran out of his office, down the corridor to the connected garage and jumped into his little blue sports car. He shoved the key into the ignition and listened to the engine roar to life, but a wave of horror, injustice and just plain fear rolled over him, and he lowered his head to the steering wheel. "Not again, Lord," he said, his words broken. "I can't go through this again."

Yet in his heart he knew that was exactly what was going to happen. He was going to watch another woman who got involved with him die.

Driving to his private airstrip, he told himself not to think like that. He told himself to stop reliving the past that had held him a prisoner for two long years. Fear had kept him in bondage for so long he didn't know how to think of anything but the worst. He knew it was because the worst had happened to him. It was logical for his thoughts to go that way. Logical. Not necessarily correct. The truth could be very different from the fears racing through him. He would feel foolish if he got to the hospital and found Sadie sitting on a bed in the emergency room, eating Jell-O, yelling to the nurses that she wanted to be released.

A tiny ray of hope lit in the darkness of Troy's soul.

If he could picture her demanding to be released, he could believe everything would be okay.

When Nigel landed the helicopter on the hospital rooftop, Troy jumped out and raced to the door. Security met him, ushered him in and informed him Sadie was in surgery. They gave him directions to a waiting area near the operating room.

Troy ran to the room and pushed the door open with a burst of nervous energy. Sadie's parents were seated in two blue plastic chairs along the back wall. Luke sat on Lilly's right, comforting her. Hannah and Caro were on their father's left, comforting him.

Troy scrambled over. "How is she?"

Pete looked up. His eyes were filled with tears. His face was drawn and colorless. "We don't know yet."

Troy's tiny hope began to vanish. "We don't know yet?"

"She's in surgery."

Troy nodded. "Okay. That's what they told me when I landed."

"Troy, sit," Luke said, rising from his plastic chair to offer it to Troy. One of Jake's high school football teammates, Luke was tall and athletic. Blond hair brushed his forehead. His green eyes were serious. "Everything's going to be fine."

Troy grabbed the statement like a lifeline. "Do you know something?"

Luke shook his head. "No."

"Then how do you know everything's going to be fine?" Despair filled him. Pain nearly paralyzed him. It was all happening again.

Hannah rose. "We know Sadie's going to be fine because she is a very strong person." She took Troy's arm and guided him to sit. "Where are the girls?"

The fact that he could be so easily put into a chair highlighted his weakness and filled Troy with a sense of impotence he couldn't bear. He stood again. "Joni and Jake stayed with the twins. And they have bodyguards...."

Bodyguards. Troy had spent the past two weeks looking for places his girls could go unattended, looking for ways they could all travel and live their lives without someone looking over their shoulders. He was integrating them into what Sadie considered a normal world, and now here they were. Just like two years ago when his wife insisted she couldn't stand the bodyguards anymore and their lives had to go back to normal.

Hadn't he learned this lesson two years ago? Didn't he know better than to believe he and his loved ones could be safe without protection? Yes. Yes, he did. But he wanted freedom so much—he wanted *Sadie* so much—that he had thrown caution to the wind, and now he was sorry. He was very, very sorry. Because he knew better.

Furious with himself, he combed his fingers through his hair. Bruce unexpectedly entered the waiting room. He caught Troy's gaze, and Troy knew exactly why he had come.

Troy faced Sadie's parents again. "Where's Chief Marshall?"

Swallowing hard, Lilly looked up. "He's on his way."

"To ask questions about the accident?"

Pete shrugged. "Probably more for moral support."

"He's not going to investigate this?" Troy asked incredulously.

"I guess they investigate every accident to a degree."

Recognizing Sadie's father hadn't considered the possibility that Sadie's accident wasn't an accident, Troy interrupted him. "It's okay. Not something we need to think about right now." *Not something her family needs to think about right now,* Troy thought as he pulled out his cell phone, *but something I have to think about and control.*

Before Troy dialed, the chief came barreling into the waiting room. "How is she?"

Sadie's father rose as the chief approached him. "She's in surgery."

Chief Marshall took off his hat and combed his fingers through his thinning brown hair. "Damn it! Damn it! Damn it! I can't believe this."

"Can you tell me exactly what happened, Chief?" Troy asked calmly, casually gathering preliminary information for the team Bruce would hire to investigate. But all his nerve endings were on fire. This was his fault. He knew it was his fault. He knew better than to let his loved ones wander about without protection.

The chief shrugged. "Her car went off the road. Our best guess is she swerved to miss a deer or a rabbit or something. The bad part is that we didn't find her until this morning."

Troy's knees almost buckled. She had wrecked her car driving from *his* house. He wanted desperately to fall to a chair, but he didn't. Instead, he said, "The bottom line to this is that she ran off the road."

"No," the chief said. "The bottom line to this is that by the time we got there she had lost a lot of blood."

Troy swallowed hard, then motioned for Bruce to leave, knowing he would understand the unspoken instruction to put together a team to investigate.

"Right," Troy said, turning to the chief. "The bottom line is that no one found her because she was alone."

And she was alone because Troy had let her be alone. Even if she hadn't been forced off the road by someone trying to get to Troy, even if it really had been an accident, if she died, it would be Troy's fault.

But he was sure this wasn't an accident. At least thirty people had seen them together at the diner. By dinner time everybody in town would have known they had a personal relationship. Anybody could have followed her to his house. Anybody could have suspected they were romantically interested in each other. And that made her a commodity. A potential kidnap victim. A way for some creep to get money. A way for someone with a political agenda to get noticed.

And Troy had let her drive alone.

When Sadie woke the next day, she could barely open her eyes. Forget about lifting her head from the pillow. She saw her parents seated on chairs by her bed and said, "What happened to me?"

"You were in an accident," Troy said, and appeared opposite her parents, both of whom leaped off their chairs and clutched her hands.

"Don't you remember?"

She tried to shake her head and couldn't. She whispered, "No."

"Think, Sadie. Think really hard," Troy said, squeezing her fingers.

But Sadie couldn't think. All she wanted to do was sleep. Her vision was blurred. Her eyelids were heavy. So she let them droop closed.

When she awakened again, the room was filled with sunshine. Her mother was sleeping on a chair. Her dad wasn't around. Troy stood staring out the window.

"Can I have some water?"

Troy spun around and walked toward her. "Ice chips are better," he said and scooped a few from a disposable cup with a plastic spoon, then slid them into her mouth. "I have to call the nurse," he said, retracting the spoon. Bending over the bed, he kissed her forehead, then smiled at her and added, "You woke once before for a few seconds, and we didn't get the nurse in the room on time to check you out. They were a bit miffed."

Sadie tried to return his smile, but couldn't. With ice chips on her tongue she also couldn't talk, so she nodded. Troy hit the buzzer for the nurse.

"I would like to transfer you out of here when you're feeling better."

Still enjoying her ice, Sadie closed her eyes. All she wanted was more sleep. She wasn't going anywhere.

"It might be safer."

She opened her eyes and tried to convey her confusion over that comment with her expression, but wasn't sure it worked. Then three nurses bustled into the room. They shooed Troy away. One ran to the bank of machines on the right side of her bed and began checking numbers. One examined Sadie's eyes and asked a few questions. One took Sadie's vitals. By the time they were done, Sadie was exhausted. She closed her eyes without another word.

When she awakened the third time, it was night again. Troy was sleeping on a chair. Her parents were gone.

"Where are Mom and Dad?" she asked, pleased that her voice sounded strong and almost normal.

Troy bounced from his seat. "Sadie!"

"Hey. Why are you here? Where are the girls? Don't tell me you left them with Jake or Joe or I'll have to get my gun and shoot you."

"Joni's there. So is Frannie."

"Oh, that's right," Sadie said, relaxing on her pillow. "I forgot about Joni and Frannie." She drew a long breath that hurt her rib cage. "I feel hideous."

Troy laughed, leaned over and kissed her forehead. "I don't doubt it."

"I probably look hideous, too."

"No. To me, you look wonderful. I especially like the blue color around your left eye."

"Such a charmer."

"You know me." He smiled warmly. Happiness emanated from his perfect blue eyes, and Sadie remembered that he had asked her out. He finally liked her. Or finally realized his life didn't have to be lonely and was willing to take a chance on falling in love with her. Though he didn't yet love her, he might someday. The fact that he was here proved he cared a lot more than Sadie had known.

And that was good.

She took another breath and got ready to drift off to sleep again, but Troy squeezed her hand. "You can't go back to sleep yet. Your accident was over forty-eight hours ago. The trail is getting cold. You need to talk to my investigators."

She squinted at him. "Investigators?"

"Sadie, there were no skid marks. It looks like you just drove off the road and hit the tree deliberately. Since we knew you were crazy but not quite nuts enough to slam into a tree, the only reason any of us could think of that you would do that was that someone ran you off the road."

She shook her head slightly. "I swerved to miss a deer."

Troy stared at her. "You hit a tree to miss a deer?"

"Yeah. That's what happens when you live in the woods. Your neighbors are of the four-legged variety, and they don't follow the same road rules the rest of us do. I swerved to avoid the object in front of my car, but I went too far, and my tires caught the gravel and I couldn't get control again."

Troy continued to study her. "You swerved to miss a deer?"

"Yes!"

"Are you sure?"

"The sucker had a horn span the size of a small state. I will remember him to the day I die."

"There was no other car?"

She shook her head. "There was no car. Only wildlife, and one of them tried to kill me."

Looking exhausted and bewildered, Troy raked his fingers through his hair. He began to turn away, and Sadie caught his hand.

"What's wrong?"

"I just thought someone had run you off the road."

Her eyes narrowed. There was only one reason she could think of that he would be this upset. "You thought someone tried to kill me," she corrected, watching him.

He drew a long breath. "Yes."

"Well, you are in luck, because it was nothing so heinous. And now we can get on with our regularly scheduled lives."

Troy shook his head. "I don't think so."

Panic welled in her chest. After finally getting to the place where he was willing to take a chance with her, she couldn't lose him over an accident. It wasn't fair! "Troy, don't make a bigger deal out of this than it is."

He gaped at her. "Sadie, you've driven these roads for over ten years and you've probably never had an accident. You don't think it's a coincidence that less than one day after we were seen together in the diner you had to swerve to miss something—"

"A deer—who has more right than you and me to be in that woods, I might add—jumped in front of my car."

He turned at the window and faced her. "I know this all looks like coincidence to you, but Bruce and I don't take chances."

She stared at him, counting to ten, giving him the benefit of the doubt because he had probably been scared. Doing her best to be objective, she said, "Okay. Let's not panic and make any rash decisions. Not only was my accident a very normal occurrence, but you were probably frightened. We shouldn't jump to any conclusions because of a deer."

Troy laughed. "This isn't about a deer, Sadie. It's about my life. It's about the fact that by getting involved with me you become a target. Terrorists could see you as a way to get money or as a way to keep me from helping our government with a special project. Opportunists could kidnap you. Wackos could hold you hostage or hurt you because they think I have a software monopoly."

"But—"

He spun to face her. "But what? Don't you see that one full day didn't even pass before you were hurt? I don't happen to believe that's a coincidence. Neither does Bruce!"

Shocked by the vehemence in his voice, Sadie rested her head against her pillow.

Troy was immediately contrite. "I'm sorry."

"I'm sorry, too, but Troy, I'm not sure I understand what you're getting at."

"I think you're going to need some protection, Sadie."

She gaped at him. "What?"

"If we're going to date, you have to have a bodyguard."

"I can't have a bodyguard! I'm a policewoman! What's he going to do? Ride with me in the squad car?"

"Either you get a bodyguard, or there can't be any us."

For a few seconds Sadie studied him. When he didn't as much as blink, she knew he was deadly serious. "I would have to give up my job. Change my entire life," Sadie whispered. "That's not fair."

"You want to talk about not fair," Troy said, walking to the bed and leaning over until he was hovering above her. "Not fair would be losing two women, two unbelievably wonderful women, the very same way. I won't go through that again, Sadie."

"Your wife was killed in an automobile accident?"

"My wife was killed in an automobile accident caused by a robbery attempt," Troy said, pacing away. "She was in her SUV. Witnesses said a van drove up behind her at a high rate of speed, then got beside her. The SUV was new, and she wasn't quite accustomed to it. When the van started sideswiping her, nudging her to pull over, she lost control."

Confused, Sadie stared at him for a few seconds, then said, "That doesn't sound like a robbery attempt."

"One of the guys involved had been our gardener. He admitted Angelina had been targeted because he knew she would have money and also because he knew she didn't have any security." He shook his head as if angry with himself. "We wanted to live normal lives."

"You still can."

"I can't!" Troy shouted, his words echoing through the room.

Sadie relented. "I'm sick, and you're exhausted. We'll talk about this later."

"We have talked about it now, Sadie. I have tried living with almost no protection for the people that I love." He paused and shook his head with disgust. "Actually, I've tried it twice. The first time I lost my wife. The second time I almost lost you. I will not ever let anyone I love go without protection again."

"Troy, I can't live like that!"

"And I can't live any other way."

Seeing he was serious and she wasn't going to

change his mind, Sadie was consumed by hopelessness. It hurt worse than the physical bruises and abrasions. But this wasn't the first hurdle for them. This was the final, unequivocal proof that a relationship between them wasn't going to work.

She licked her dry lips. "Troy, I'm really serious when I say I can't live like that. I spent the first weeks I was home feeling like I was in hell because of some gossip. A little courage and wit got me out of it. I won't go into another prison."

"It's not a prison."

"How can you say that? How can you of all people say that!"

"Because I choose to see the bright side."

"I don't see a bright side. And it's not how I can live."

"Sadie, like you said, we're both tired. Tomorrow…"

"Tomorrow I will feel the same way. Tomorrow, the next day, the next day and the next day I will want to have a life." She squeezed her eyes shut. "I would prefer that you were in my life with me, but you can't be. You can't be in my life."

He shook his head. "No," he said, then swallowed hard. "I can't. I want you to come live with me in mine."

She shook her head. "I can't."

He drew a long breath but didn't say anything. Pain radiated from his eyes, but his body was stiff, rigid. She could see from his expression that he wanted nothing more than to take what she was offering, to have the life she believed they could have. But the reality was he knew he couldn't.

She knew he couldn't.

"Then this is it."

Without another word, he scooped his jacket from the back of the chair and headed for the door.

"Troy..."

He turned.

"I'm so sorry." She could feel tears welling in her eyes, and pain that had nothing to do with her injuries ricocheted through her.

"I'm sorry, too." He pressed his lips together, taking a minute to compose himself, then said, "If you don't mind, I'm going to have Bruce keep track of things here for a day or so."

"It was an accident, Troy."

He nodded. "I know. Just humor me."

"Okay."

"Okay," he said and pushed open the door, but he stopped and faced her again. "I never told you this before because I thought it was too soon, but I love you, Sadie. There will never be another you."

He walked through the door, and it swished closed behind him.

Tears cascaded down Sadie's cheeks. He had finally said what she wanted to hear, that he loved her. He had been afraid it was too early to say it, but oddly enough, it was too late.

Chapter Eleven

Troy instructed Bruce to stay with Sadie, and returned home. The second he stepped into the foyer, the twins pounced. "Dad! How's Sadie? When's she coming home? Will she be sick here? Will we take care of her?"

In spite of his pain, Troy smiled and stooped to catch them in his arms. "Girls, Sadie isn't sick. She was in an accident and because of that she needs to stay in the hospital."

"Can we visit her?"

Troy looked at Frannie. Frannie shrugged nonchalantly. "I don't see why not."

"Okay. If Frannie says you can visit, you can visit. But there are a couple of things you need to know."

"Like no noise," Jake said, coming into the foyer. "Hospitals are very quiet places."

"Well, actually, it would be better for you guys to wait to visit Sadie until she's out of the hospital," Troy said. "I understand she's being released day after tomorrow. So if you can wait two days, then you can visit her at home.''

The twins nodded enthusiastically, so eager to see Sadie it was pitiful. Troy's heart sank. His next piece of news would hurt them almost as much as it hurt him to say it.

''There's one more thing.''

Both girls blinked at him.

''Sadie and I kind of...well, we're not going to be friends anymore.''

''You're not going to be friends?'' the girls asked, obviously confused.

''You're not going to be friends?'' Jake asked incredulously.

''You're not going to be friends?'' Joni asked, walking into the foyer.

''Before the girls visit Sadie, they need to know that Sadie's not going to be part of our lives the way we hoped she would, but that's as far as our discussion goes. I don't want to talk about it.''

Frannie put her hands on the girls' shoulders and directed them up the steps. ''How about if we change into swimsuits and go outside for some fresh air.''

The girls gave their dad an odd look but didn't argue. When they were gone, Joni caught Troy's arm and forced him to face her. ''What happened?''

Troy sighed. ''I told her I thought the accident proved I had to go back to having full-time protection, and if she and I wanted to date, that meant she had to have protection, too. She refused.''

''She refused? Just like that? No argument, no explanation?'' Joni asked, obviously confused.

''Of course we argued. And of course we both had

our own explanation for why we were right. There was no point of compromise.''

''So you broke up with a woman in the hospital and you're okay with that?''

Troy stared at her. ''Of course, I'm not okay with it! But Sadie doesn't like the way I live, and I can't change that. This is nobody's fault!''

Though he expected Joni to apologize, she drew a quick breath, pivoted and left the foyer as if Troy had been the one in the wrong.

Troy worked for two days straight. Partially to catch up with projects that had fallen behind while he waited for Sadie to wake up in the hospital, partially to avoid having to defend himself. It would have been okay to explain his position to his friends and family if he felt better about it. But he didn't. He hurt the whole way to his soul, and no one seemed to understand that. Against his better judgment he had fallen in love with a woman he couldn't have, and it crushed him to lose her.

Troy's twins confirmed their lack of understanding when they returned, sobbing, from visiting Sadie the following Sunday. Joni was furious with him. Frannie was pointedly silent. Even Jake appeared to be changing sides.

Angry with everyone in his life, Troy didn't say a word. Instead, he slammed his way to the garage and jumped into his old truck. He only drove the battered and rusty vehicle when he was feeling out of sorts. It was as far removed from the state of his life as anything could be. And right now he felt like he needed to get away from his life.

He didn't take issue with everybody seeing Sadie's

side. What annoyed Troy was that everybody acted as if being stubborn about protection and losing the woman he loved was somehow easy for him. No one seemed to understand that he was lonely, too. He wanted to love Sadie. He *needed* Sadie, but he couldn't have her in his life at the risk of her life, his life or the lives of his children.

Not sure where he was going, Troy shoved the gearshift into reverse to get out of the garage, then he wreaked havoc with the transmission, grinding gears the entire way down his driveway. For fifty cents he would get himself on a highway, head south and never be heard from again.

Except he couldn't do that to his daughters. With that thought he slowed, made a quick right turn and headed to the old country cemetery. Only a few minutes later, he found the thin dirt lane that took him to Angelina's grave. Because of the old-fashioned setup of the cemetery, he could drive to within a few feet of the grassy plot.

He parked the truck and jumped out, glad he had made the choice to have her laid to rest in Wilburn instead of L.A.

When he reached her grave he folded his hands, calmed his nerves, said a prayer and waited. With his eyes closed and his mind quiet he heard a flock of birds flying overhead, cows mooing and a train in the distance. He took a short breath as the peace of the September afternoon flooded him.

He no longer heard Angelina's voice when he visited. He knew that had been a manifestation of his own grief, so he wasn't surprised that as his grief lessened her voice disappeared. Just like he wasn't surprised that two minutes by her side calmed him down.

Opening his eyes, he drew another breath, then lovingly ran his hand long the heart-shaped curve of the gravestone. "You would adore the girls," he said, dropping to the ground, taking a seat beside her. It suddenly occurred to him that he hadn't visited since bringing Sadie into his life. He didn't think it odd that he hadn't told Angelina about Sadie, but it didn't seem right not to tell her what was going on in the twins' lives.

"They're very happy. Believe it or not, they've been to the local day care, and I enrolled them in my old school. Wilburn Elementary…"

He stopped, realizing that in spite of Sadie's accident it had never occurred to him to take the twins out of Wilburn Elementary.

"Actually, I can't take credit for enrolling the girls," he continued, knowing he could think later about why he hadn't returned the girls to Briarhills. "Sadie talked me into it. Sadie is the woman I hired to help me point the girls in the right direction."

He paused. Angelina wouldn't let him lie.

He cleared his throat. "Sadie is Sadie Evans. She was helping because I bribed her dad," he said, and felt much better for it. "But I was desperate. You remember the day I was here telling you about the snakeskin hip huggers and the pink feather boas? That same day I saw Sadie arresting a kid for shoplifting, but doing it nicely, and right then and there I not only knew she had grown beyond her great ambition of marrying a rich man, but I also realized I needed a woman's help with the girls. I tried to talk her into working for me, but she refused. So I offered her dad a hundred thousand dollars, which I would pay to Pete

Evans's ailing sister and her day care if he could convince Sadie to work for me.''

He shook his head. "I know. I know. That's management one-oh-one. How to manipulate people. We swore we would never be that way." He shook his head again, and chuckled. "But it worked."

He lay back on the grass, propping himself up on his elbows and gazing at the sky, recognizing that he finally felt good, felt right, because this was where he belonged.

"Anyway," he said. Staring at the sky, he saw that one cloud looked like Larry King. "I might have bribed her dad, but the truth is, her aunt really needs the money, so in the end everybody was getting what they wanted."

He paused. The world was so quiet he could hear the September breeze ruffle through the trees, and he remembered it was Sadie who had taught him how to see pictures in clouds. She taught him how to relate to his daughters. She made him feel as if he again had a partner, someone who understood him and his life. And he had lost her.

He swallowed hard. "Actually, not everybody got what they wanted. Sadie... Well, Sadie is a very beautiful woman. And I was... Well, I was very attracted to her." He laughed. "I'm still attracted to her. But I didn't really pursue her. Falling in love just sort of happened. I wanted everything from her, but I recognize the restrictions of my life. I was always honest with her about why a relationship between us probably wouldn't work. I didn't lead her on."

He drew a long breath. "That's why I'm so mad at Frannie and Joni. They're furious with me. They think I hurt her, but I didn't hurt her. I wouldn't ever hurt her. She's wonderful. She helped the girls. She changed our lives. She made me laugh again.''

"She made me laugh again,'' he whispered, gazing at the cloud that looked like Larry King. The cloud beside it was clearly a toaster. The one beside that was a snow cone.

He glanced at the gravestone and swallowed hard. "No, she didn't make me laugh as much as she made me look at everything differently. And *that* made me happy.''

He squeezed his eyes shut. "Oh, Angelina, I see what happened. She straightened out my perspective of life. She made me see I didn't need so many body-guards and that I could send the kids to the local school.'' He squeezed his eyes even tighter. "But the first time I was tested, I failed.''

Birds chirped. Cows mooed. The breeze rustled the trees. Troy let the knowledge that he had failed settle over him. That was the real truth. It wasn't the changes in his life that had failed. His faith had failed. *He* had failed.

"I failed,'' he said, hoisting himself from the ground. "I don't think I've ever failed a test.'' He laughed slightly. "I guess this is how the other half lives. I gotta tell you, Angelina, this trial and error stuff is hell.''

He kissed his fingers the way he always did and pressed them to the gravestone. "I better go find Sadie.''

Sadie hadn't ever been more miserable in her entire life. Still bruised from her accident, she was confined to her parents' house to heal. She couldn't work. She missed the twins. Their visit that day hadn't helped. It only reminded her that she missed them…and their father.

Every time she thought about Troy, pain squeezed her heart. After she saw the girls, the pain was so intense she knew she couldn't lie around the house thinking about him. There was no point to pondering that he finally, finally loved her but she couldn't have him. She had to do something. It wouldn't be something foolish like beg him to reconsider his lifestyle. The fears he had were understandable and deep-rooted. But her need to lead a normal life was every bit as deep-rooted.

She hoisted herself off the sofa, hit the remote control to silence the TV and headed upstairs to change. Though she couldn't wear anything beyond sweatpants and a T-shirt, that was progress over pajamas.

She knew she couldn't drive to Pittsburgh, but she was fairly certain that if she got cranky enough Luke would happily take her there. She didn't have a job or an apartment, but she had a friend she could stay with, and she knew the department would take her back. She couldn't remain in Wilburn, watching Troy's daughters grow up, watching Troy be miserable. It would kill her.

She crept down the quiet hall to the kitchen. She would wait for Luke to come in from the backyard. He and her dad were watching football under the huge corner oak tree, but she couldn't make it that far on her own. Plus, she wouldn't coerce Luke in front of their dad. Pete Evans would never let his daughter return to Pittsburgh like this. She had to catch Luke alone, when he ran into the house for more beer.

She hobbled to the window, dragging a lightweight kitchen chair because she couldn't stand for any length of time. Then she shifted the curtain to the right an inch so she could watch her dad and Luke, and get ready to pounce when Luke raced in for more beer. Five minutes passed, with her father and Luke hooting and hollering and cheering, but beyond a quick swig, neither of them looked very interested in beer.

Drat.

"Do you know that in some countries, Peeping Toms are hanged?"

Sadie swung away from the window. "Troy! What are you doing here?"

"Saving you from a life of crime."

It was so good to see him Sadie's breath caught, and all she could think of was that he was here because he had changed his mind. But that was impossible. She knew the depth of his fear. She had heard it in his voice. If he wasn't here to beg her to come back, she wasn't sure she wanted to hear the real reason he had come. She decided to delay the inevitable and stick with the teasing. "Ha! I'm a police officer. Someday I'll probably be saving your twins from a life of crime."

"So you're staying in Wilburn?"

Filled with shame because her flippant answer had led him on, Sadie looked down. "No, Troy. I'm not staying. In fact, if I can coerce Luke, I'm going back to Pittsburgh today."

"Wow." He fell to one of the kitchen chairs. "Then I guess I'm just in time."

"Just in time?"

"I'll need to get account information from you so that I can transfer that hundred thousand dollars to your aunt's day care."

Tears stung Sadie's eyes. Though she knew she

shouldn't have been disappointed he hadn't returned for her, that tiny flicker of hope had nonetheless built inside her, and misery swamped her.

"I'll get it."

She began to hurry from the room, but bruised and battered, she couldn't move quickly. Her progress was slow and awkward. Troy easily caught her hand as she tried to get by him. Already off balance, she fell to his lap when he tugged on her fingers.

Before she could say anything, he nuzzled his face in her neck. "I'm sorry."

She had no clue what he was sorry for, but right at the moment she was filled with remorse and regret, too, and her tears spilled over. She didn't want to go to Pittsburgh. She was worried about his daughters. Worried about him. No matter how much she tried to convince herself returning to Pittsburgh was the right thing to do, her life felt out of sync, and it didn't seem fair.

She ran her fingers through his hair and whispered, "I'm sorry, too. But this is just one of those things that isn't ever going to work out...."

"Now, see, there's where we disagree." He caught her roaming fingers and brought them to his lips. "Because I think if we compromised we could make this work."

She stared at him. "I thought you didn't want to compromise."

"I was wrong."

She waited for him to give her details, and when he didn't, she said, "Damn it, Troy. Say something. Explain this."

"I went to Angelina's grave this morning and I had

a conversation with myself, a cow, a flock of birds and a cloud that looked like Larry King."

"A cloud that looked like Larry King?"

"It was the cloud that looked like Larry King that made me realize I had panicked. I was so afraid of trying again that the first time our new situation was tested, I thought it failed. But the truth was I failed."

"*You* failed?"

"I panicked. I thought the worst. I didn't look at the facts. I jumped to all the wrong conclusions."

"Troy, it didn't sound like you panicked to me. You seemed to understand that your life is different. You need protection."

"Yes and no. The other thing I figured out this morning was that even after your accident, I didn't return the girls' lives to what they had been. I let them keep their friends, and they still go to Wilburn Elementary. Bruce doesn't follow them around. Neither does Frannie. She shuttles them and supervises them, but she doesn't go everywhere they go. I didn't change their lives back to what they were because deep down inside I knew they didn't need to go back."

"I see."

Troy shook his head. "I don't think you do. After Angelina's death, I really had gone too far in the security direction. By being the girls' helper and trying to straighten out their behavior by straightening out their lives, you showed me a lot of where I was wrong. But I didn't get all the lessons right. I have the kid thing down pat. It's my own life that needs straightening out. So now I need you to bring me the whole way back."

Her eyes filled with tears again. "Really?"

"I'm not going to live without bodyguards. There'll

always be some around. But I don't have to live in a prison, and neither should the girls... Neither should you."

She caught his gaze. "You're willing to change your life that much?"

"Oh, God, yes!" he said, burying his face in her hair. "I can't live without you, Sadie."

"I can't live without you, either."

"Then what's all this talk about moving back to Pittsburgh?"

She could tell him of her sleepless nights and despair over losing the love of her life, but gazing into his sincere blue eyes, Sadie knew that was over now, and they would never again dwell on the past. They would move into the future.

She looped her arms around his neck and bumped her forehead to his. "I was leaving because Hannah snores."

"Good save," Troy said, then he kissed her.

* * * * *

SILHOUETTE *Romance*®

Coming in April 2003, look for brand-new stories from two of Silhouette Romance's brightest stars.

A beautiful image consultant makes every attempt to ignore her heart and turn one ruggedly handsome blue-collar bachelor into

A WHOLE NEW MAN
Roxann Delaney
(SR #1658)

Confident she's put her past behind her, a sophisticated city girl returns home...and comes face-to-face with the love of her life. One look and she knows

HE'S STILL THE ONE
Cheryl Kushner
(SR #1659)

Available at your favorite retail outlet.

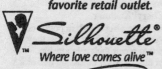

Silhouette®

Where love comes alive™

Visit Silhouette at www.eHarlequin.com   SRWNMHS

SILHOUETTE *Romance*

COMING NEXT MONTH

#1654 DADDY ON THE DOORSTEP—Judy Christenberry
Despite their fairy-tale courtship, Andrea's marriage to Nicholas Avery
was struggling. But when a torrential downpour left them stranded,
Andrea had one last chance to convince her emotionally scarred husband that he was the perfect husband and—surprise!—daddy!

#1655 JACK AND THE PRINCESS—Raye Morgan
Catching the Crown
Princess Karina Roseanova was expected to marry an appropriate suit-
or—but found herself *much* more attracted to her sexy bodyguard, Jack
Santini. Smitten, Jack knew that a relationship with the adorable
princess was a bad idea. So when the job was over, he would walk
away…right?

#1656 THE RANCHER'S HAND-PICKED BRIDE—
Elizabeth August
Jess Logan was long, lean, sexy as sin—and not in the market for marriage. But his great-grandmother was determined to see him settled, so
she enlisted Gwen Murphy's help. Jess hadn't counted on Gwen's
matchmaking resolve or the havoc she wreaked on his heart. Could the
match for Jess be…Gwen?

#1657 THE WISH—Diane Pershing
Soulmates
Shy bookstore owner Gerri Conklin's dream date was a total disaster!
She wished to relive the week, vowing to get it right. But when her wish
was granted, she found herself choosing between the man she *thought*
she loved—and the strong, silent rancher who stole his way into her
heart!

#1658 A WHOLE NEW MAN—Roxann Delaney
Image consultant Lizzie Edwards wanted a stable home for her young
daughter, and that didn't include Hank Davis, the handsome man who'd
hired her to instruct him about the finer things in life. But her new client
left her weak-kneed, and soon she was mixing business with pleasure….

#1659 HE'S STILL THE ONE—Cheryl Kushner
Zoe Russell returned to Riverbend and made a big splash in police chief
Ryan O'Conner's life—ending up in jail! Formerly best friends, they
hadn't spoken in years. As they worked to repair their relationship,
sparks flew, the air sizzled…but *when* did friends start kissing like *that*?

SRCNM0303